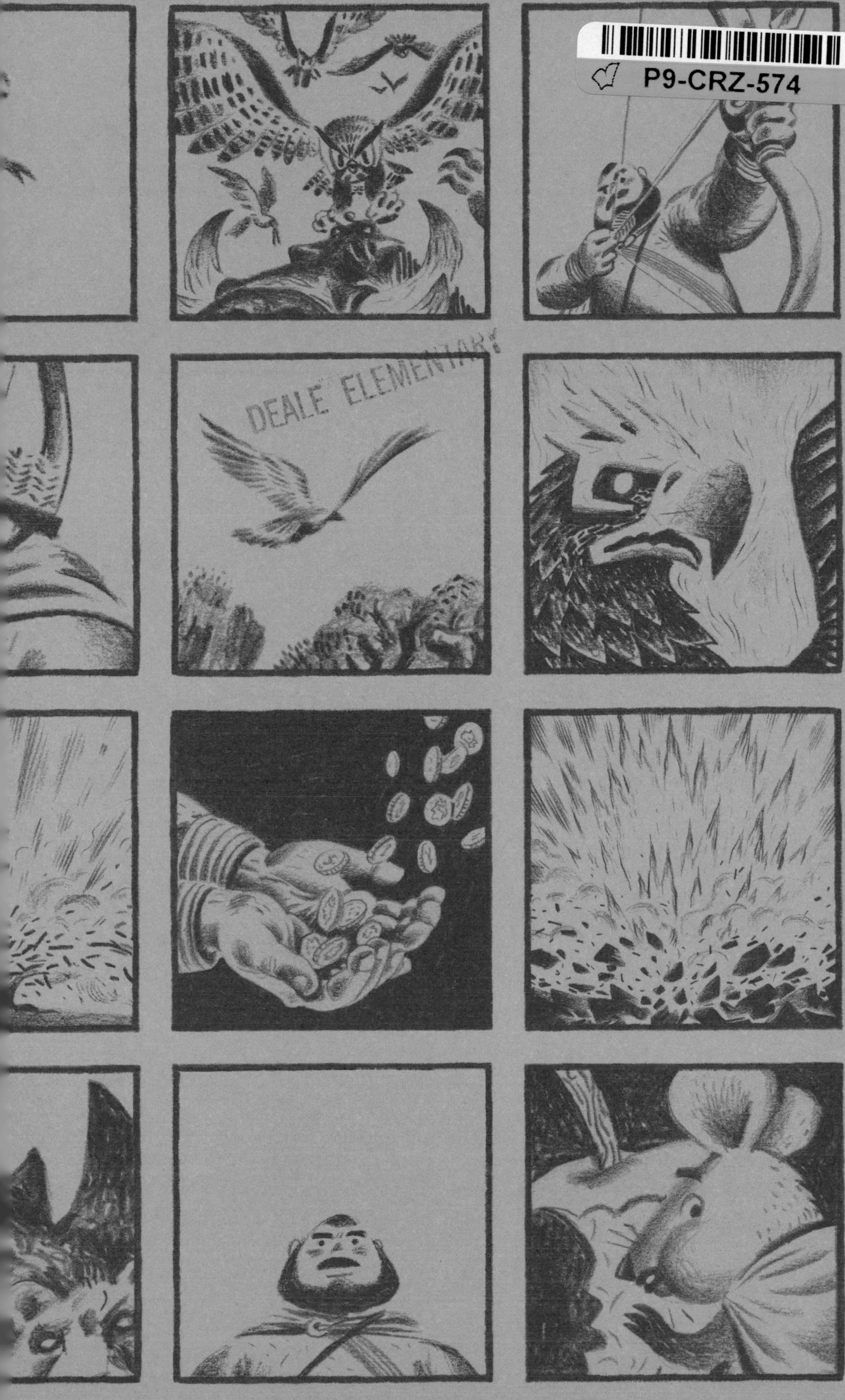

TO MY PARENTS, ANYA,
MIKE MIGNOLA & WALT DISNEY.

UTKIN

GAMAYUN
TALES

BASED ON RUSSIAN
FOLK TALES

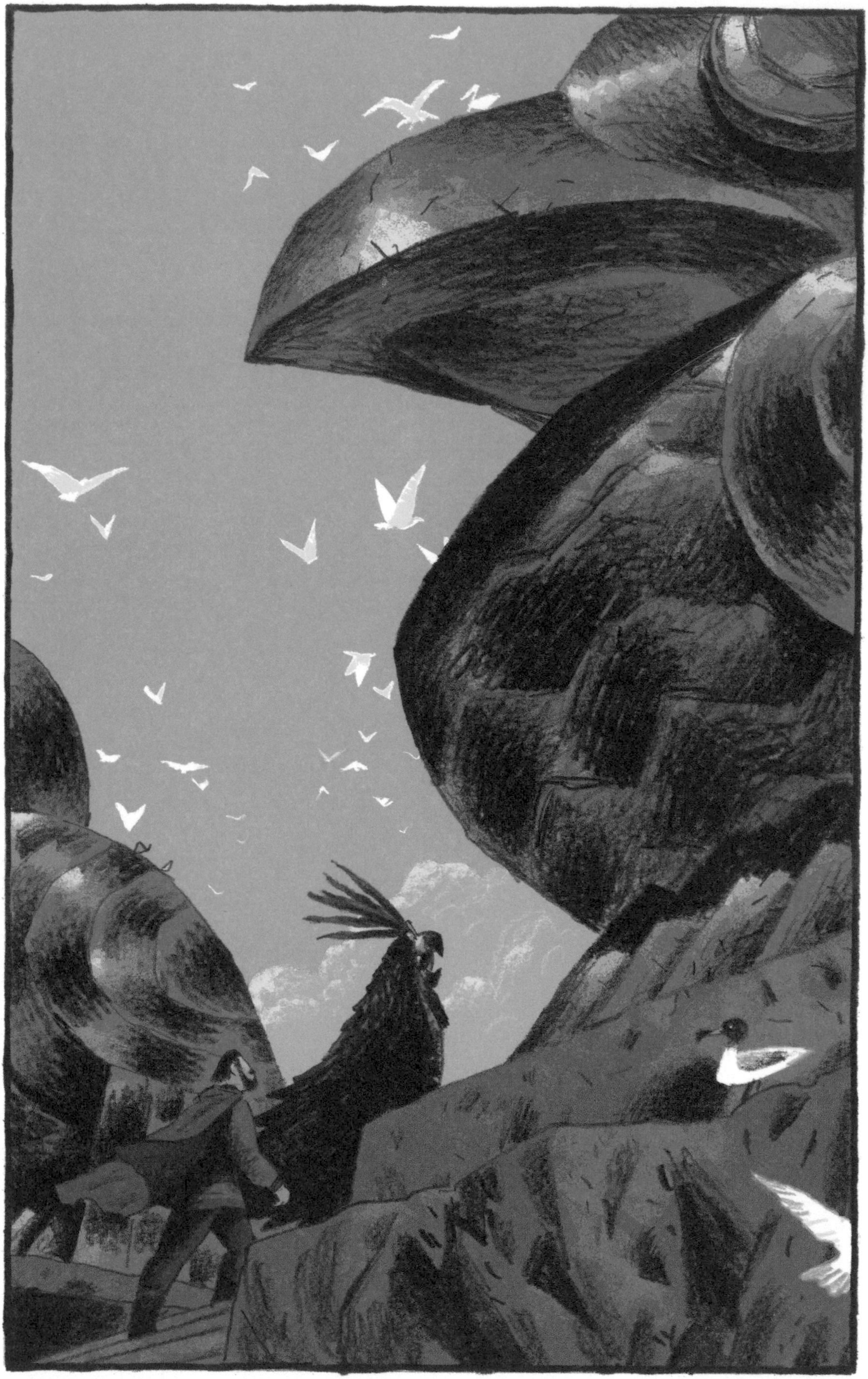

THE KING OF BIRDS

WRITTEN & DRAWN BY
ALEXANDER UTKIN

TRANSLATED BY
LADA MOROZOVA

NOBROW
LONDON | NEW YORK

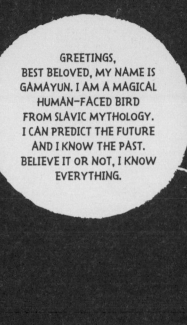

GREETINGS,
BEST BELOVED, MY NAME IS
GAMAYUN. I AM A MAGICAL
HUMAN-FACED BIRD
FROM SLAVIC MYTHOLOGY.
I CAN PREDICT THE FUTURE
AND I KNOW THE PAST.
BELIEVE IT OR NOT, I KNOW
EVERYTHING.

BUT WHAT I REALLY
LIKE IS TO TELL STORIES!
TALES OF COURAGE,
LOVE AND WISDOM.
SOMETIMES, MY TALES
MIGHT APPEAR
A LITTLE SCARY,
BUT I'D RATHER
SAY EXCITING!

YOU'LL SEE
FOR YOURSELF.
TURN THE PAGE
AND WE SHALL
BEGIN!

THE QUARREL

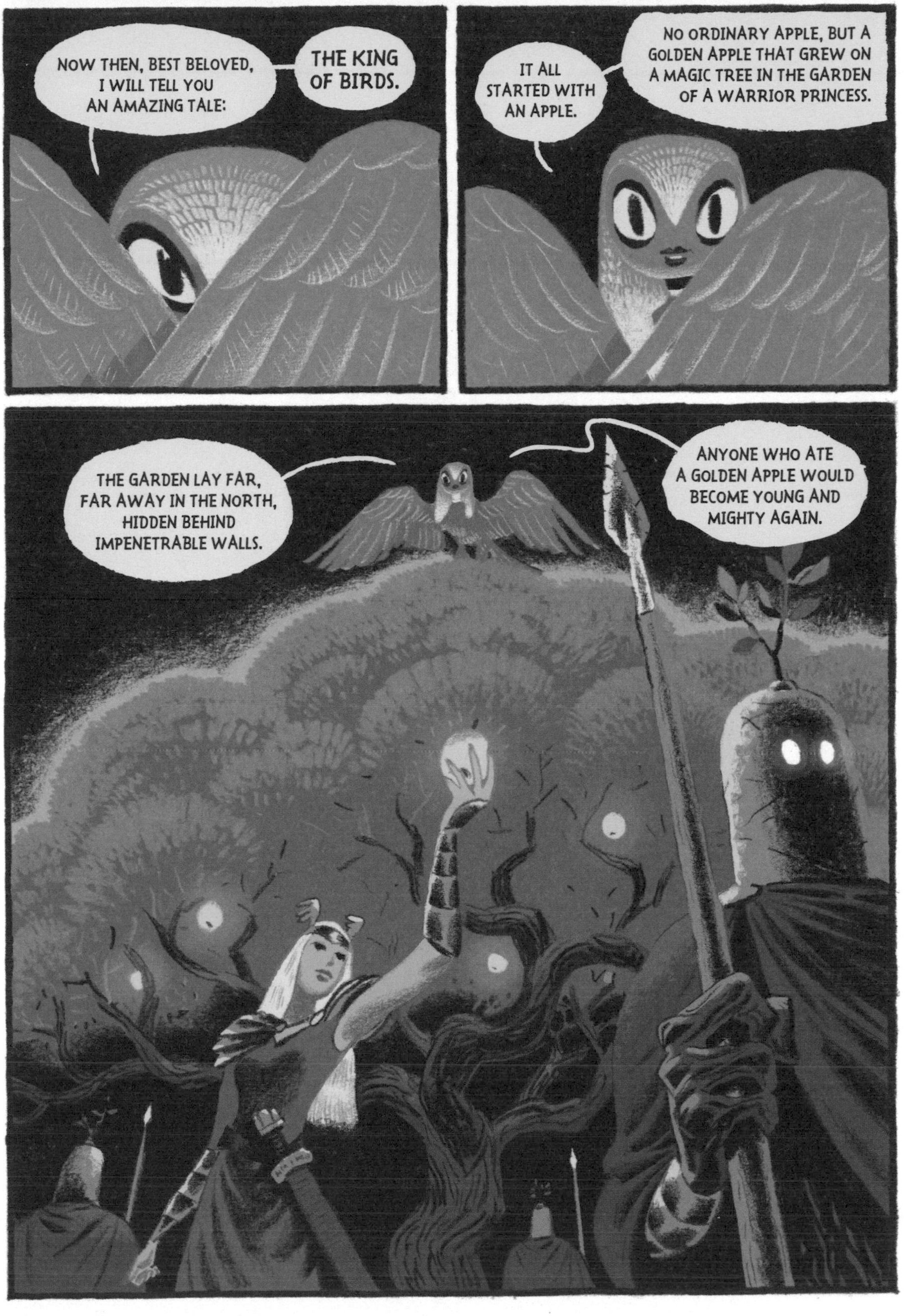
NOW THEN, BEST BELOVED, I WILL TELL YOU AN AMAZING TALE:
THE KING OF BIRDS.
IT ALL STARTED WITH AN APPLE.
NO ORDINARY APPLE, BUT A GOLDEN APPLE THAT GREW ON A MAGIC TREE IN THE GARDEN OF A WARRIOR PRINCESS.
THE GARDEN LAY FAR, FAR AWAY IN THE NORTH, HIDDEN BEHIND IMPENETRABLE WALLS.
ANYONE WHO ATE A GOLDEN APPLE WOULD BECOME YOUNG AND MIGHTY AGAIN.

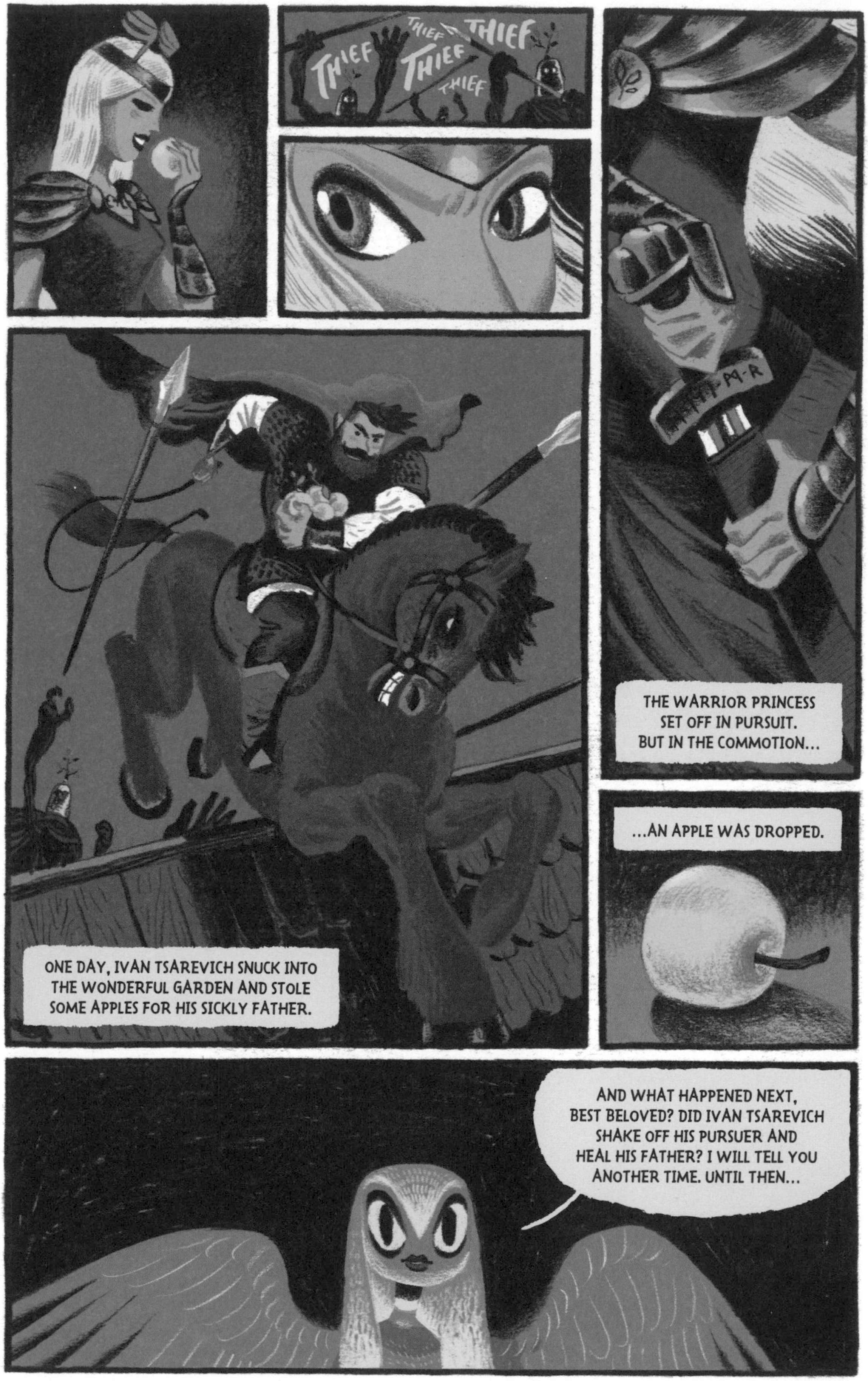
THIEF
THIEF
THIEF
THIEF
THIEF
THE WARRIOR PRINCESS SET OFF IN PURSUIT. BUT IN THE COMMOTION...
ONE DAY, IVAN TSAREVICH SNUCK INTO THE WONDERFUL GARDEN AND STOLE SOME APPLES FOR HIS SICKLY FATHER.
...AN APPLE WAS DROPPED.
AND WHAT HAPPENED NEXT, BEST BELOVED? DID IVAN TSAREVICH SHAKE OFF HIS PURSUER AND HEAL HIS FATHER? I WILL TELL YOU ANOTHER TIME. UNTIL THEN...

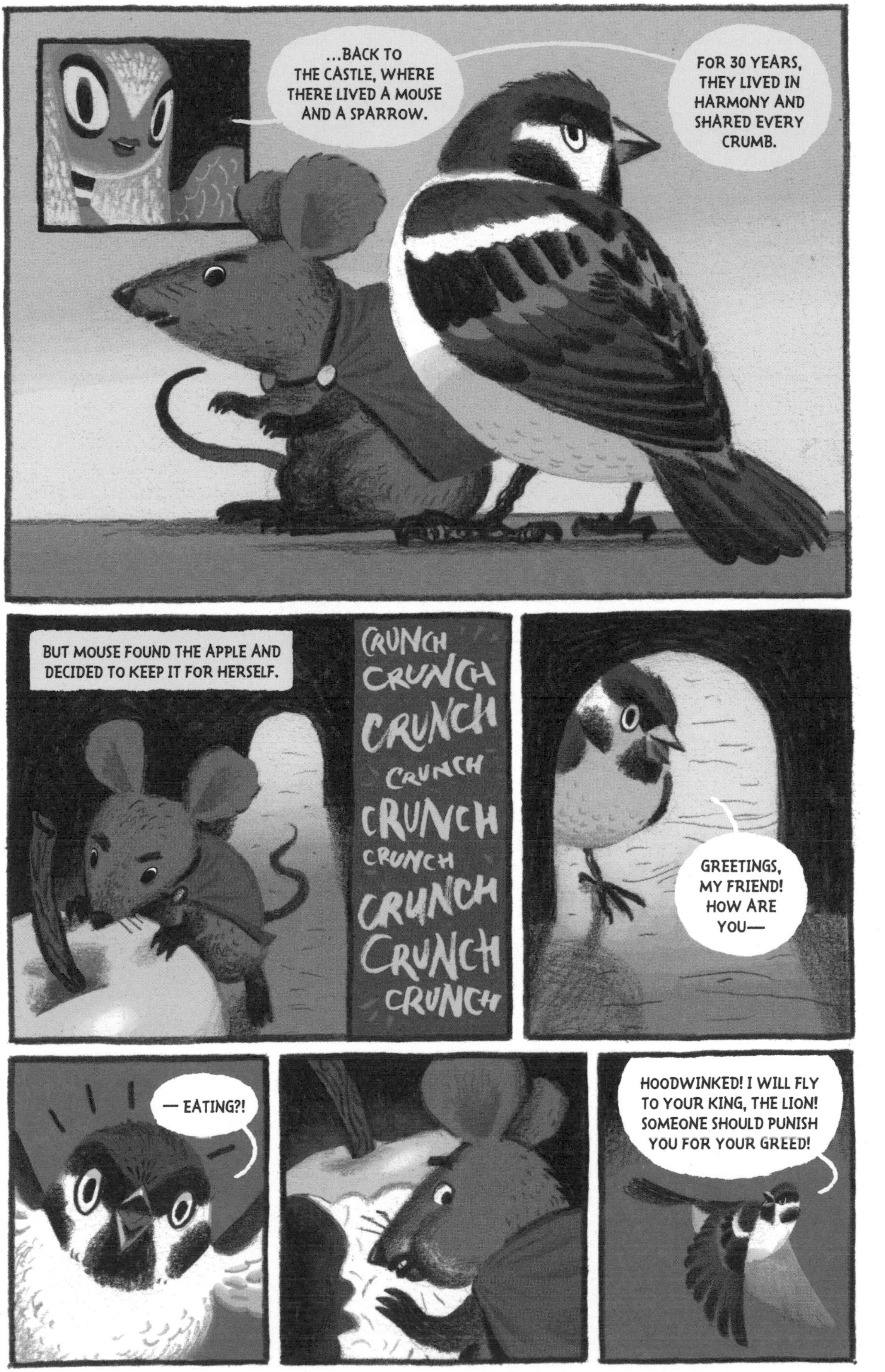
...BACK TO THE CASTLE, WHERE THERE LIVED A MOUSE AND A SPARROW.
FOR 30 YEARS, THEY LIVED IN HARMONY AND SHARED EVERY CRUMB.
BUT MOUSE FOUND THE APPLE AND DECIDED TO KEEP IT FOR HERSELF.
CRUNCH CRUNCH CRUNCH CRUNCH CRUNCH CRUNCH CRUNCH CRUNCH CRUNCH
GREETINGS, MY FRIEND! HOW ARE YOU—
— EATING?!
HOODWINKED! I WILL FLY TO YOUR KING, THE LION! SOMEONE SHOULD PUNISH YOU FOR YOUR GREED!

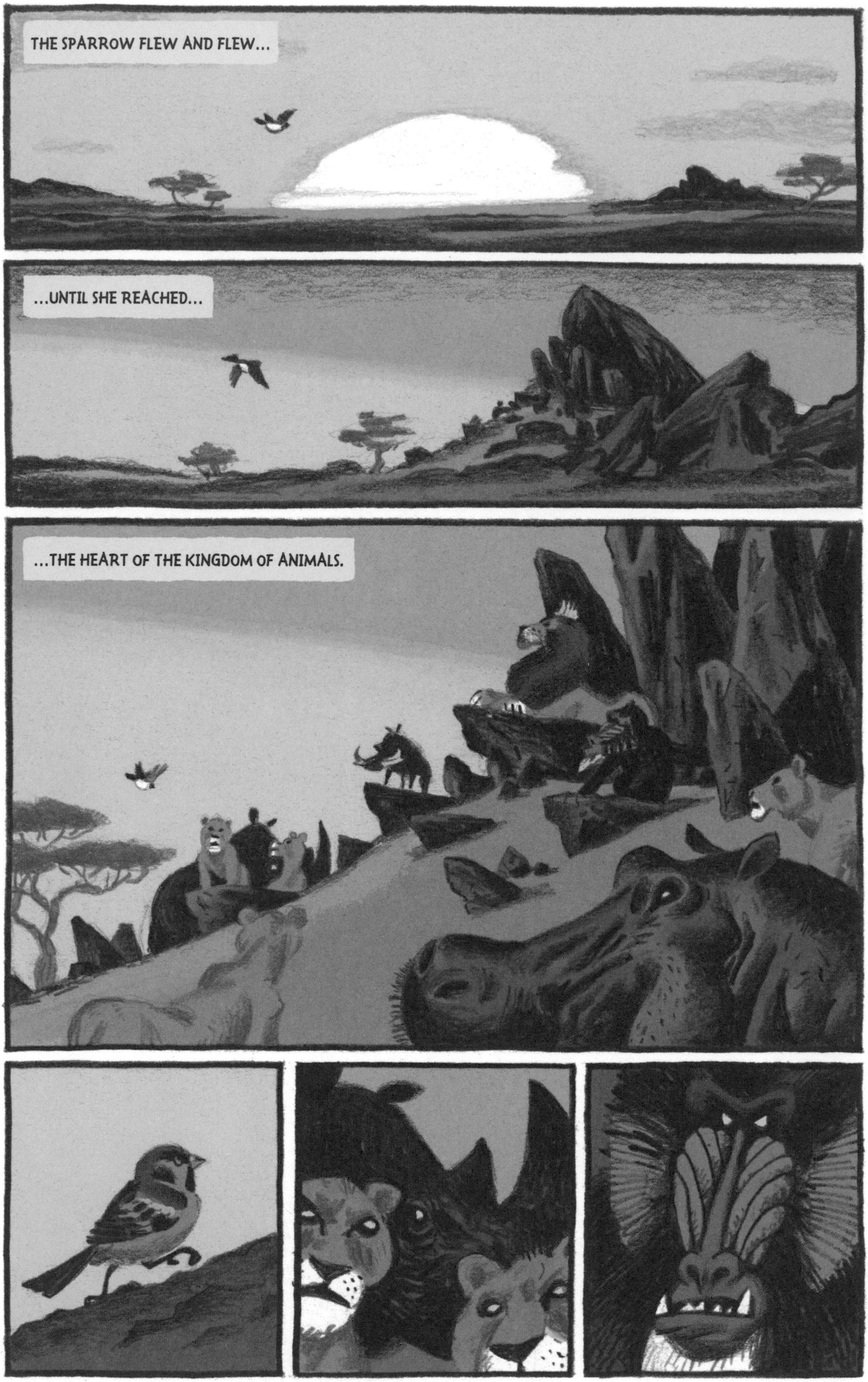
THE SPARROW FLEW AND FLEW...
...UNTIL SHE REACHED...
...THE HEART OF THE KINGDOM OF ANIMALS.

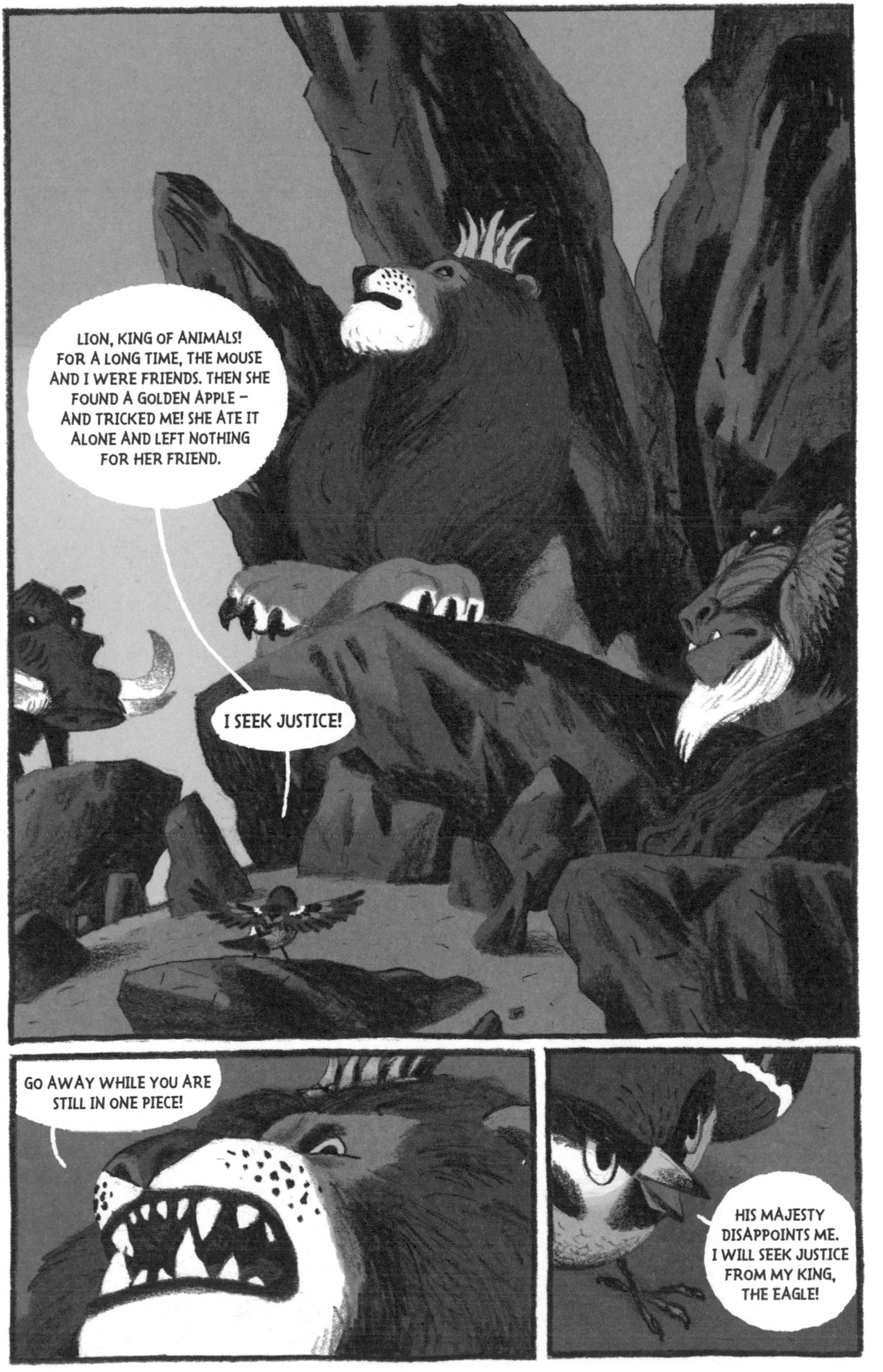
LION, KING OF ANIMALS! FOR A LONG TIME, THE MOUSE AND I WERE FRIENDS. THEN SHE FOUND A GOLDEN APPLE – AND TRICKED ME! SHE ATE IT ALONE AND LEFT NOTHING FOR HER FRIEND.
I SEEK JUSTICE!
GO AWAY WHILE YOU ARE STILL IN ONE PIECE!
HIS MAJESTY DISAPPOINTS ME. I WILL SEEK JUSTICE FROM MY KING, THE EAGLE!

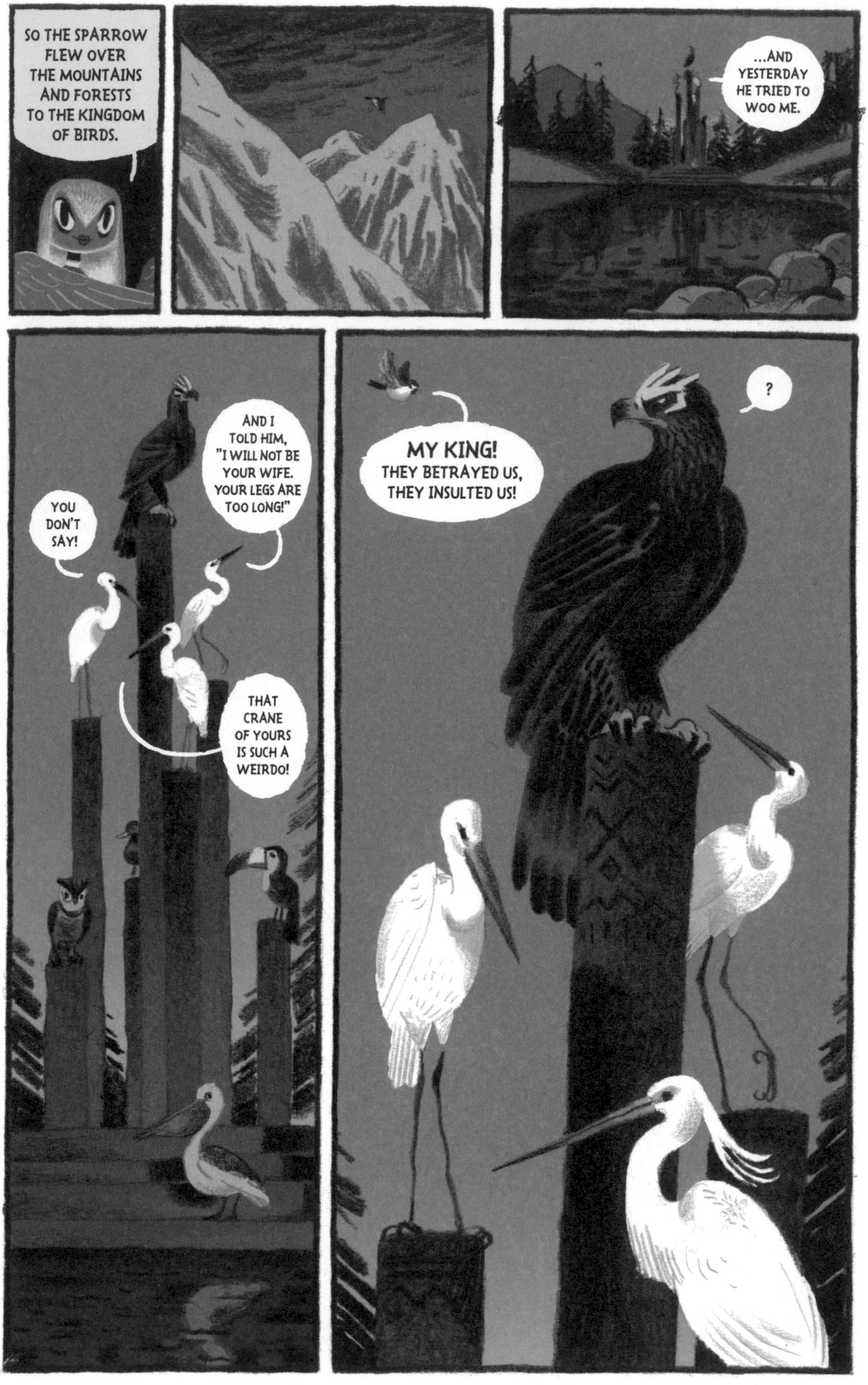
SO THE SPARROW FLEW OVER THE MOUNTAINS AND FORESTS TO THE KINGDOM OF BIRDS.
...AND YESTERDAY HE TRIED TO WOO ME.
AND I TOLD HIM, "I WILL NOT BE YOUR WIFE. YOUR LEGS ARE TOO LONG!"
YOU DON'T SAY!
THAT CRANE OF YOURS IS SUCH A WEIRDO!
MY KING! THEY BETRAYED US, THEY INSULTED US!
?

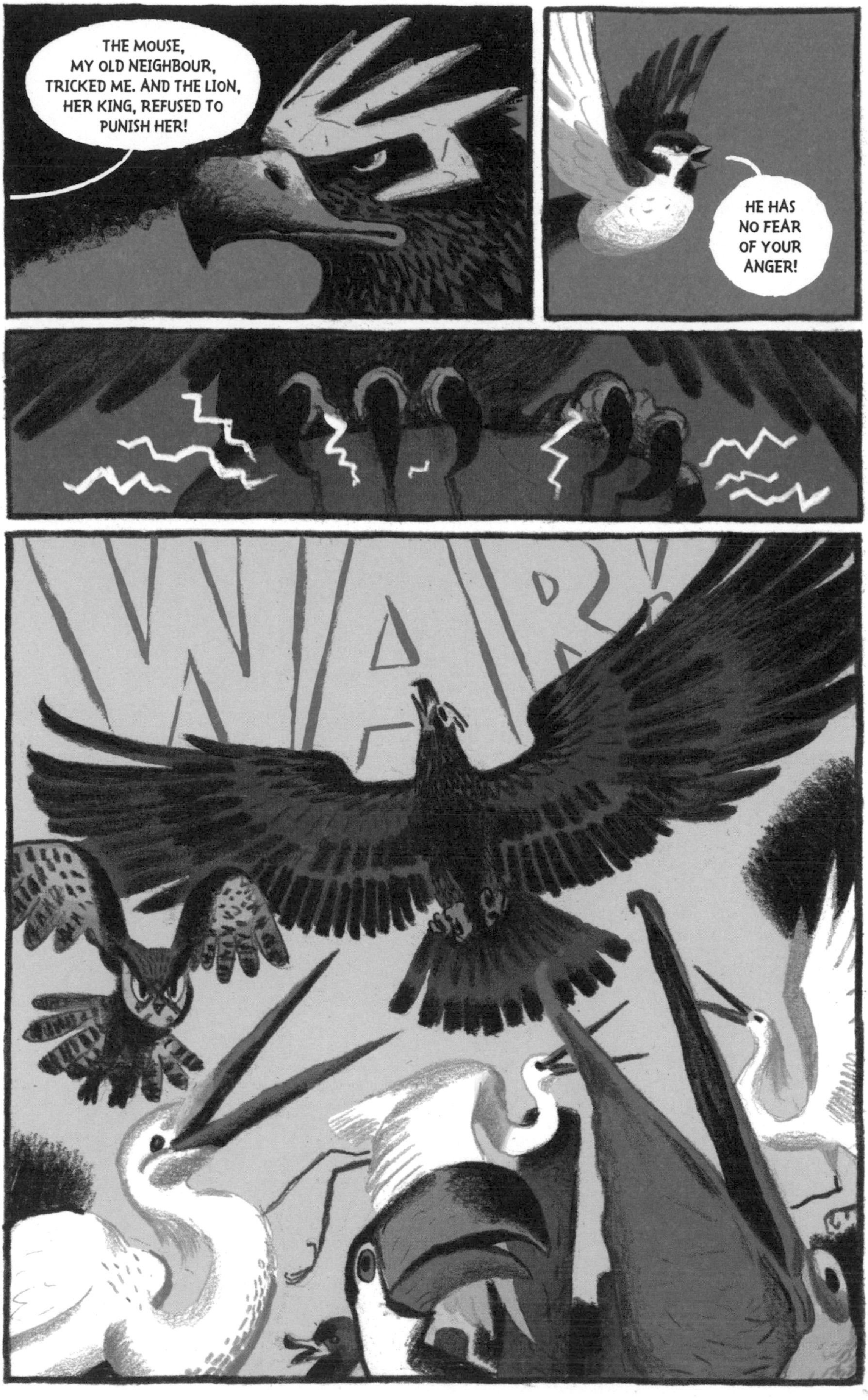
THE MOUSE, MY OLD NEIGHBOUR, TRICKED ME. AND THE LION, HER KING, REFUSED TO PUNISH HER!
HE HAS NO FEAR OF YOUR ANGER!
WAR!

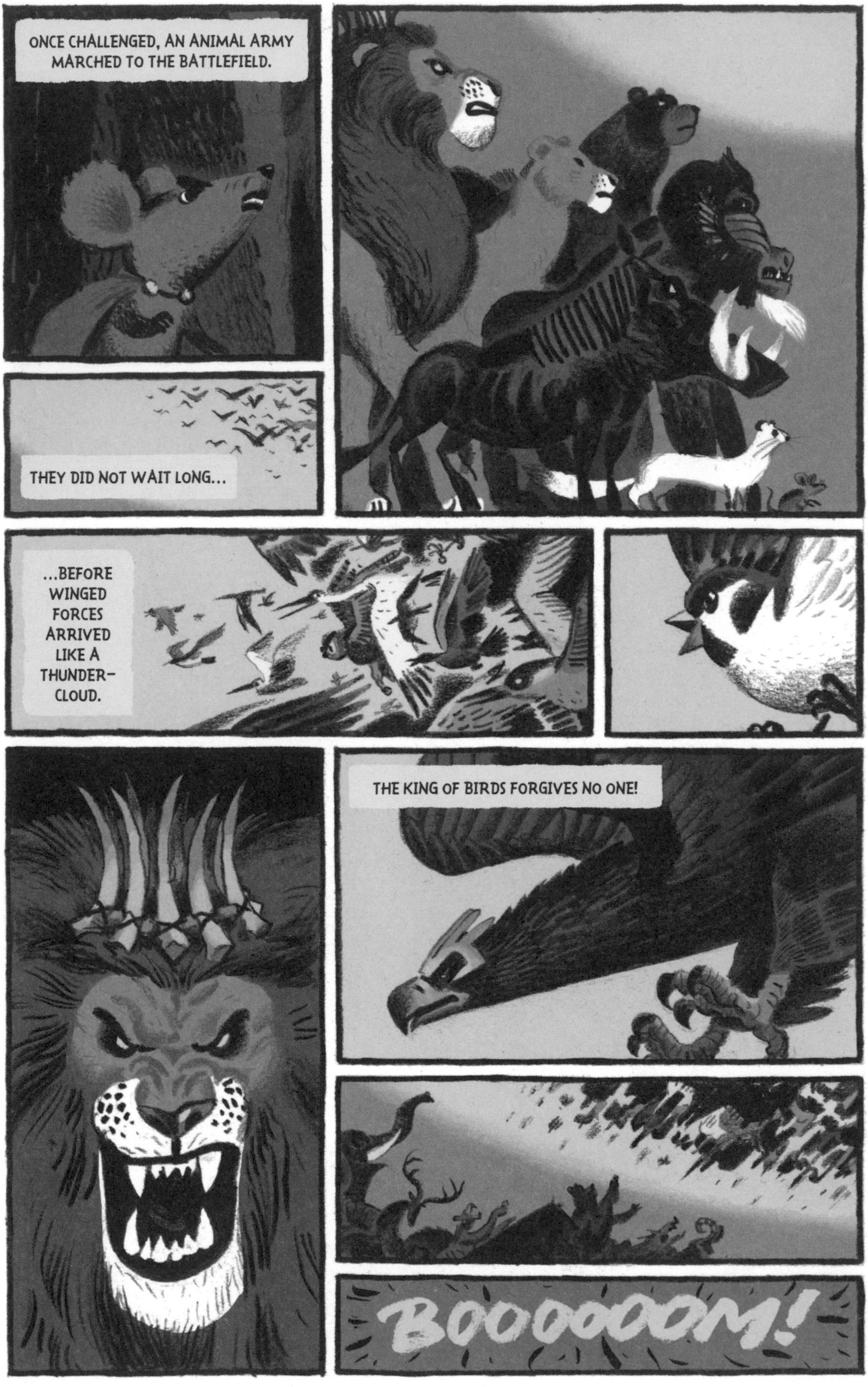
ONCE CHALLENGED, AN ANIMAL ARMY MARCHED TO THE BATTLEFIELD.
THEY DID NOT WAIT LONG...
...BEFORE WINGED FORCES ARRIVED LIKE A THUNDER-CLOUD.
THE KING OF BIRDS FORGIVES NO ONE!
BOOOOOOM!

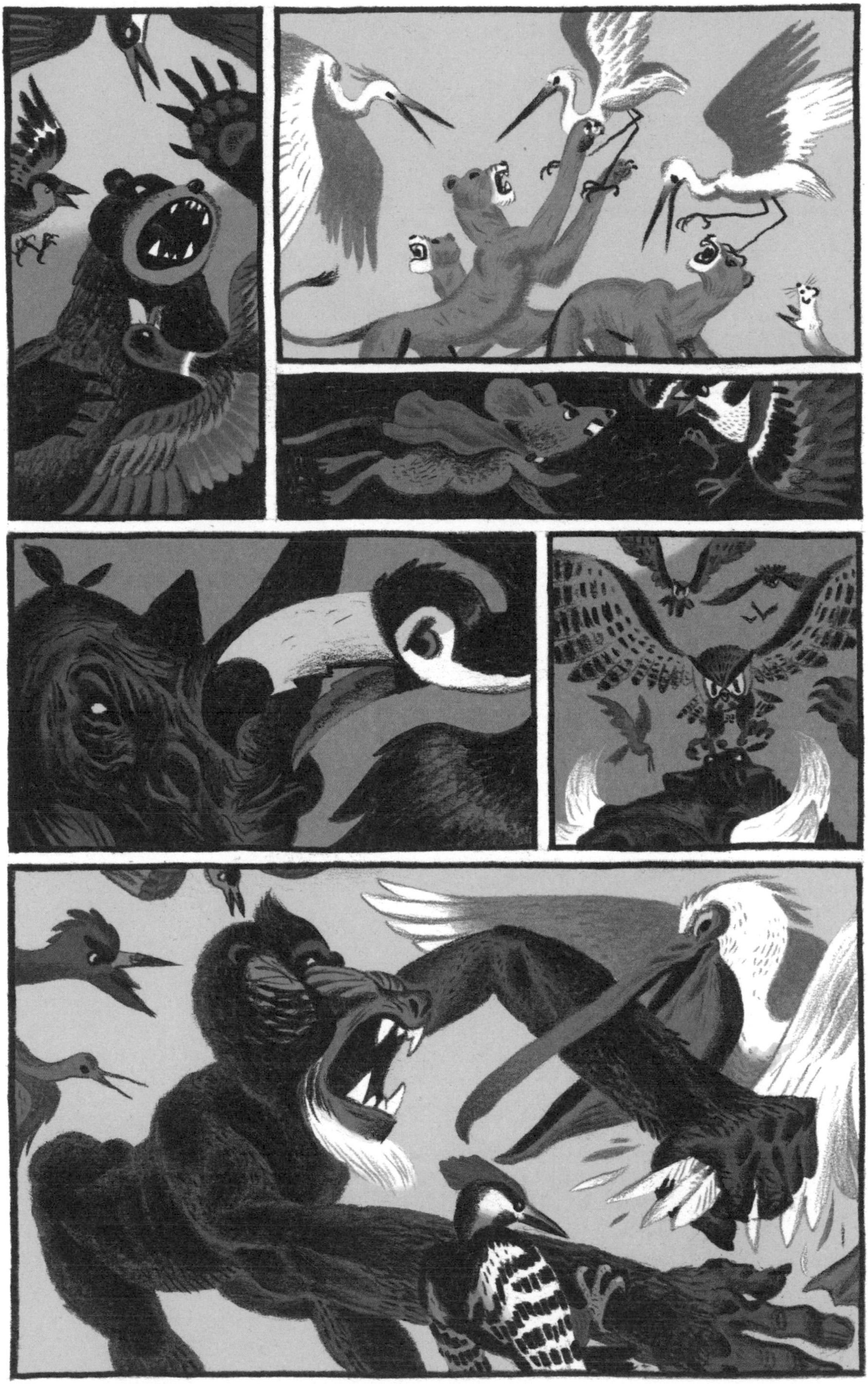

THE BATTLE RAGED FOR THREE DAYS AND THREE NIGHTS. THE ANIMALS WERE MIGHTY, YET THE BIRDS RESISTED – AND RAINED DOWN BLOW AFTER BLOW FROM THE SKY...

...UNTIL EVEN THE TERRIBLE LION GAVE IN.

AR-R-R-R!

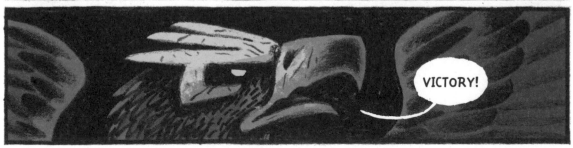

VICTORY!

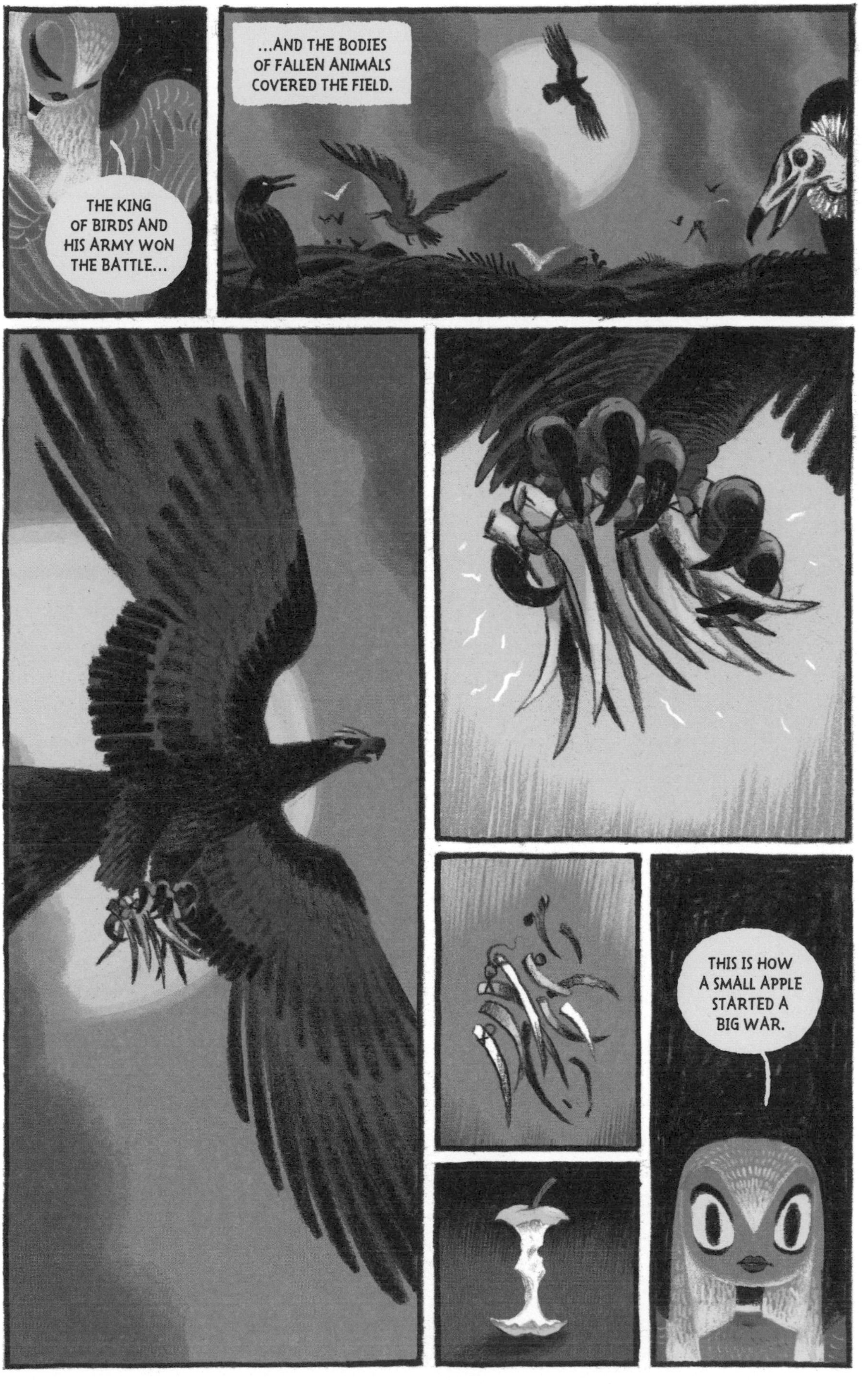
THE KING OF BIRDS AND HIS ARMY WON THE BATTLE...
...AND THE BODIES OF FALLEN ANIMALS COVERED THE FIELD.
THIS IS HOW A SMALL APPLE STARTED A BIG WAR.

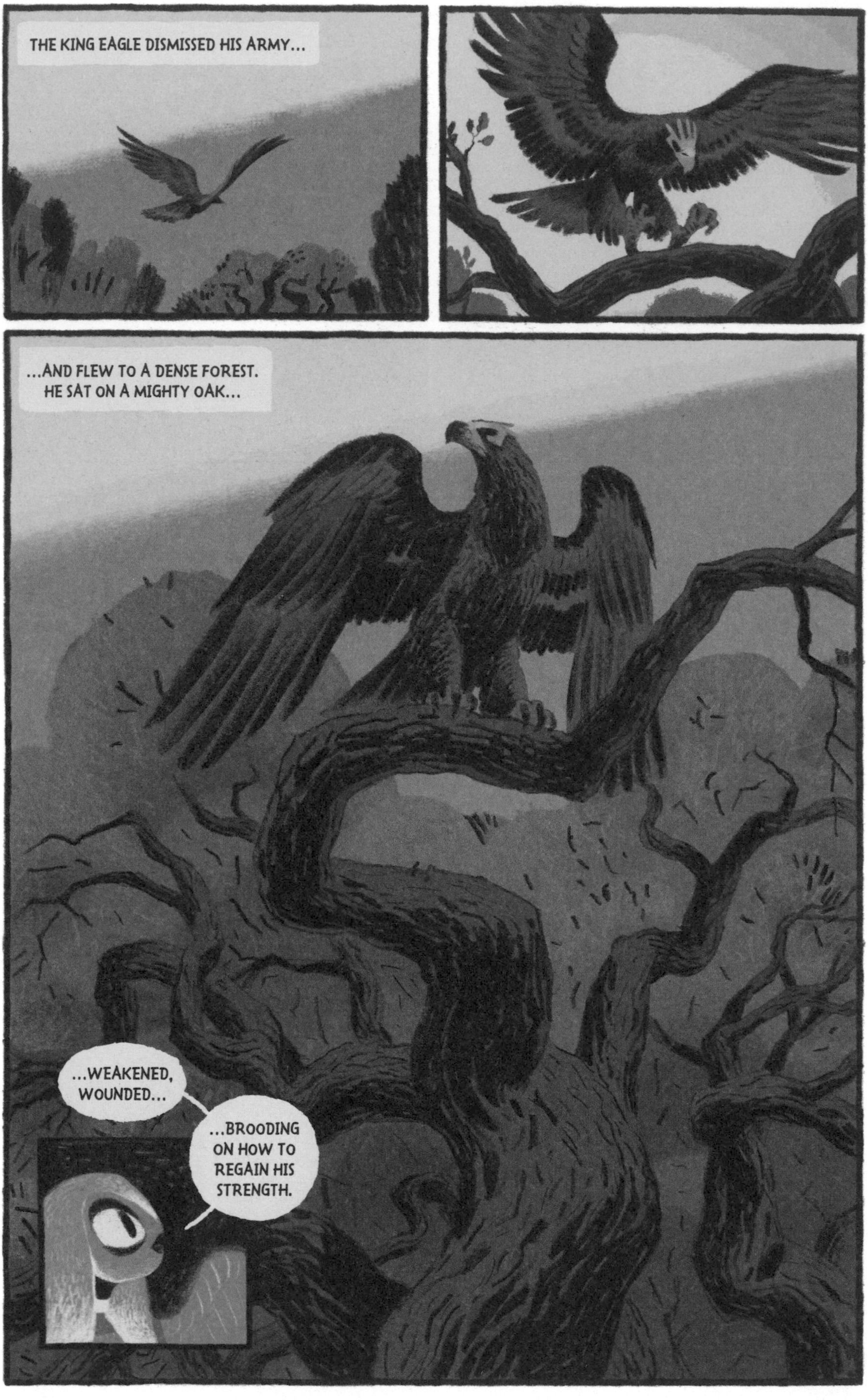
THE KING EAGLE DISMISSED HIS ARMY...
...AND FLEW TO A DENSE FOREST.
HE SAT ON A MIGHTY OAK...
...WEAKENED, WOUNDED...
...BROODING ON HOW TO REGAIN HIS STRENGTH.

THE KING OF BIRDS

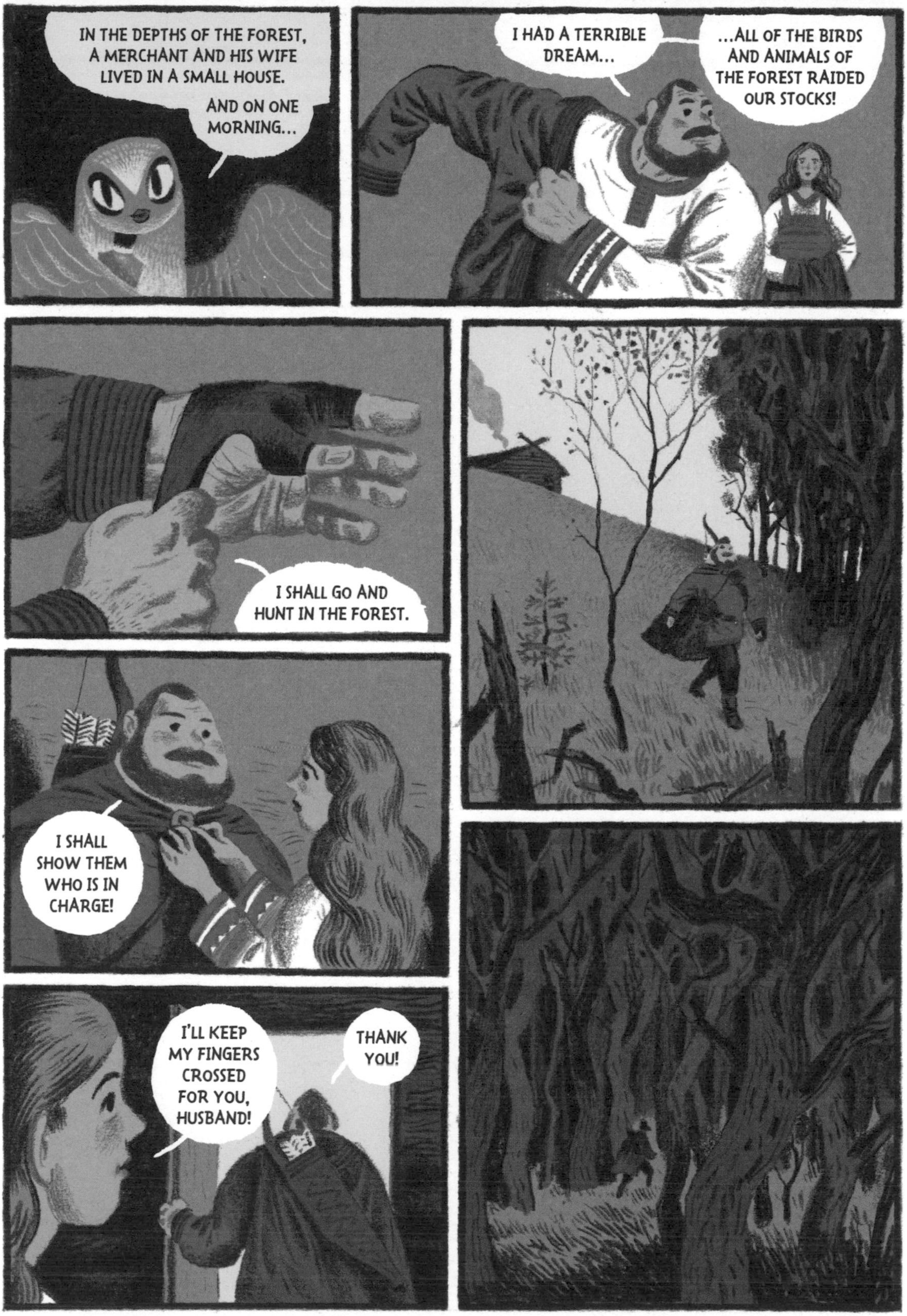
IN THE DEPTHS OF THE FOREST, A MERCHANT AND HIS WIFE LIVED IN A SMALL HOUSE.
AND ON ONE MORNING...
I HAD A TERRIBLE DREAM...
...ALL OF THE BIRDS AND ANIMALS OF THE FOREST RAIDED OUR STOCKS!
I SHALL GO AND HUNT IN THE FOREST.
I SHALL SHOW THEM WHO IS IN CHARGE!
I'LL KEEP MY FINGERS CROSSED FOR YOU, HUSBAND!
THANK YOU!

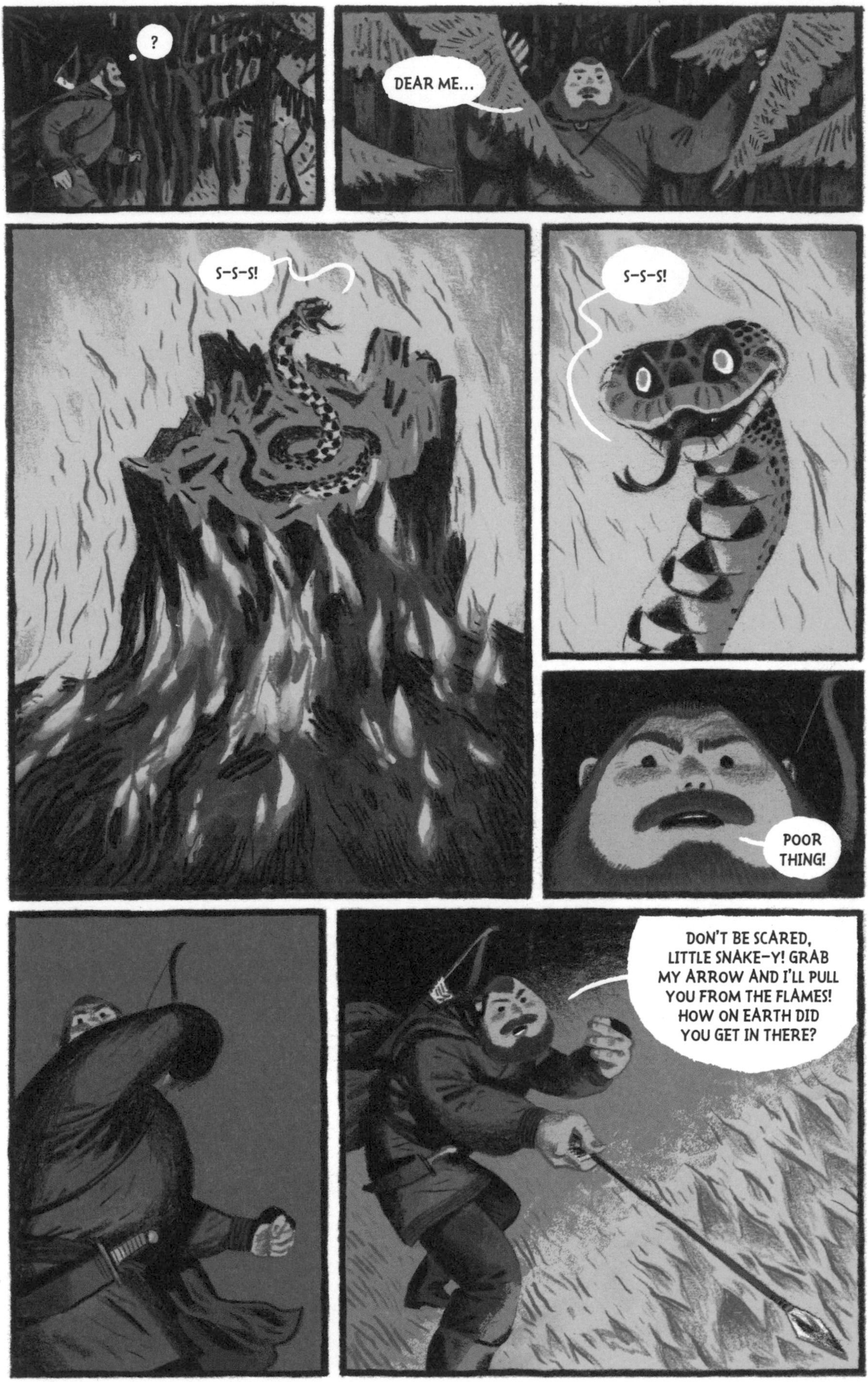
?
DEAR ME...
S-S-S!
S-S-S!
POOR THING!
DON'T BE SCARED, LITTLE SNAKE-Y! GRAB MY ARROW AND I'LL PULL YOU FROM THE FLAMES! HOW ON EARTH DID YOU GET IN THERE?

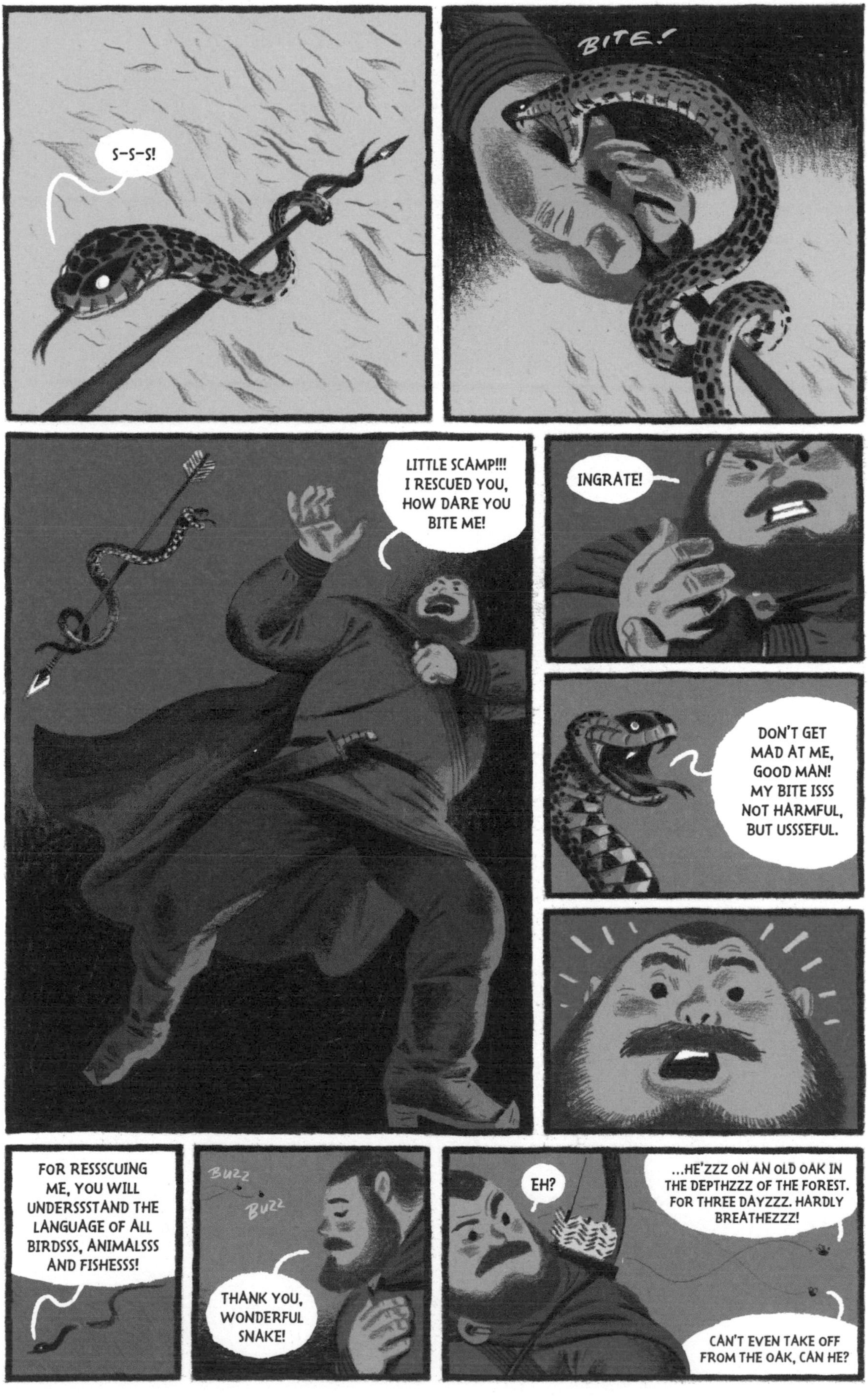
S-S-S!
BITE!
LITTLE SCAMP!!! I RESCUED YOU, HOW DARE YOU BITE ME!
INGRATE!
DON'T GET MAD AT ME, GOOD MAN! MY BITE ISSS NOT HARMFUL, BUT USSSEFUL.
FOR RESSSCUING ME, YOU WILL UNDERSSSTAND THE LANGUAGE OF ALL BIRDSSS, ANIMALSSS AND FISHESSS!
BUZZ
BUZZ
THANK YOU, WONDERFUL SNAKE!
EH?
...HE'ZZZ ON AN OLD OAK IN THE DEPTHZZZ OF THE FOREST. FOR THREE DAYZZZ. HARDLY BREATHEZZZ!
CAN'T EVEN TAKE OFF FROM THE OAK, CAN HE?

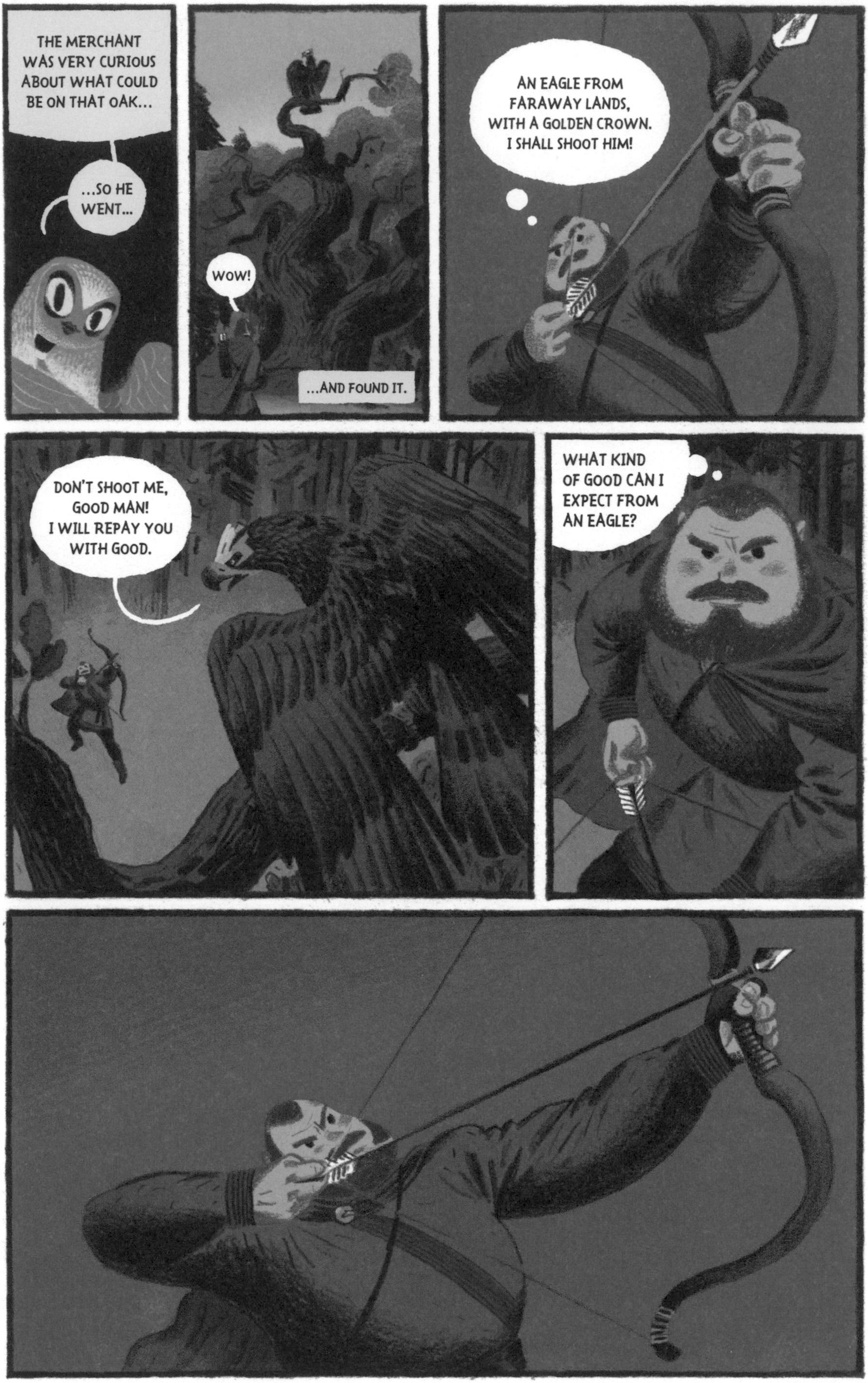
THE MERCHANT WAS VERY CURIOUS ABOUT WHAT COULD BE ON THAT OAK...
...SO HE WENT...
WOW!
...AND FOUND IT.
AN EAGLE FROM FARAWAY LANDS, WITH A GOLDEN CROWN. I SHALL SHOOT HIM!
DON'T SHOOT ME, GOOD MAN! I WILL REPAY YOU WITH GOOD.
WHAT KIND OF GOOD CAN I EXPECT FROM AN EAGLE?

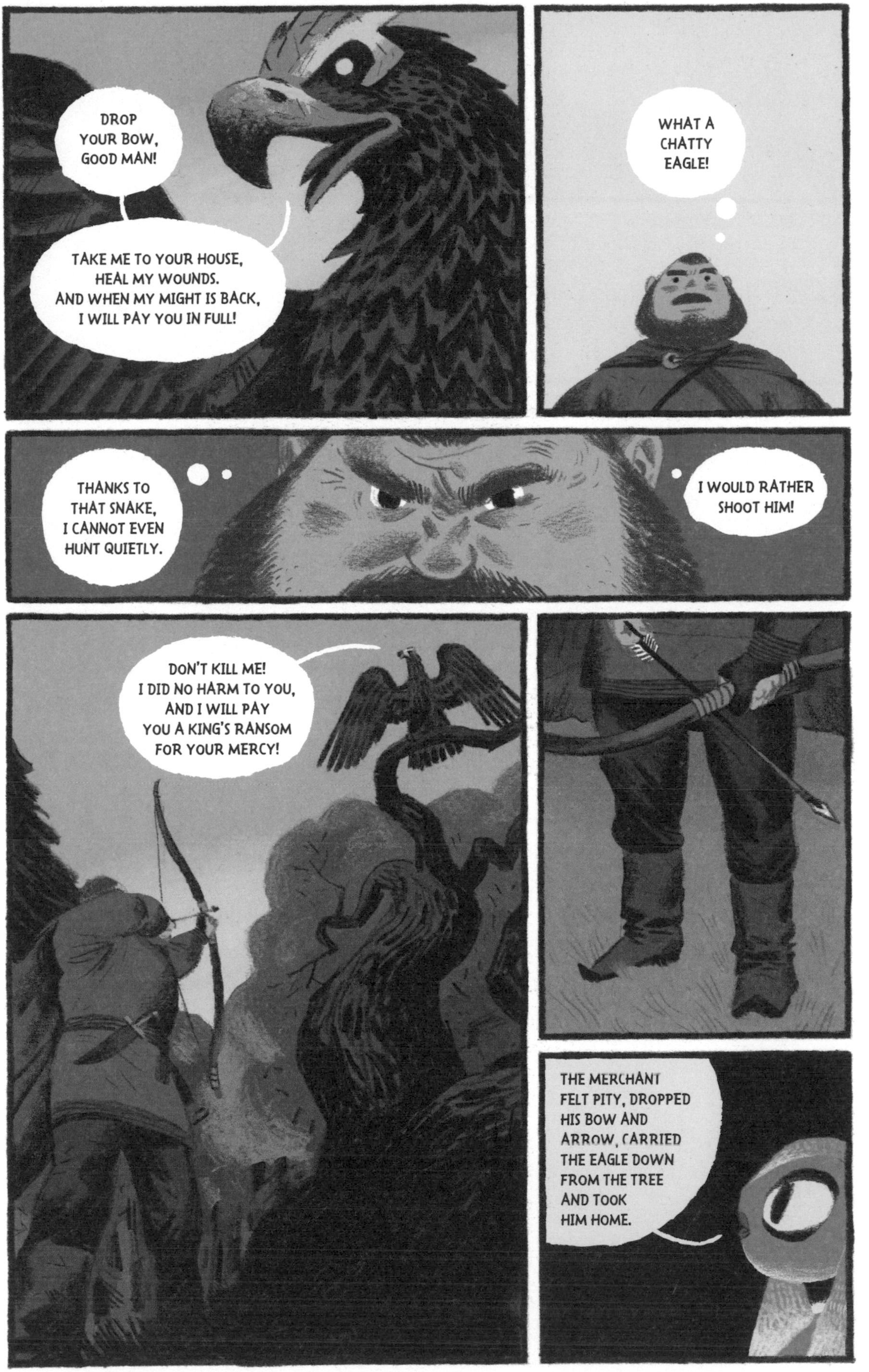
DROP YOUR BOW, GOOD MAN!
TAKE ME TO YOUR HOUSE, HEAL MY WOUNDS. AND WHEN MY MIGHT IS BACK, I WILL PAY YOU IN FULL!
WHAT A CHATTY EAGLE!
THANKS TO THAT SNAKE, I CANNOT EVEN HUNT QUIETLY.
I WOULD RATHER SHOOT HIM!
DON'T KILL ME! I DID NO HARM TO YOU, AND I WILL PAY YOU A KING'S RANSOM FOR YOUR MERCY!
THE MERCHANT FELT PITY, DROPPED HIS BOW AND ARROW, CARRIED THE EAGLE DOWN FROM THE TREE AND TOOK HIM HOME.

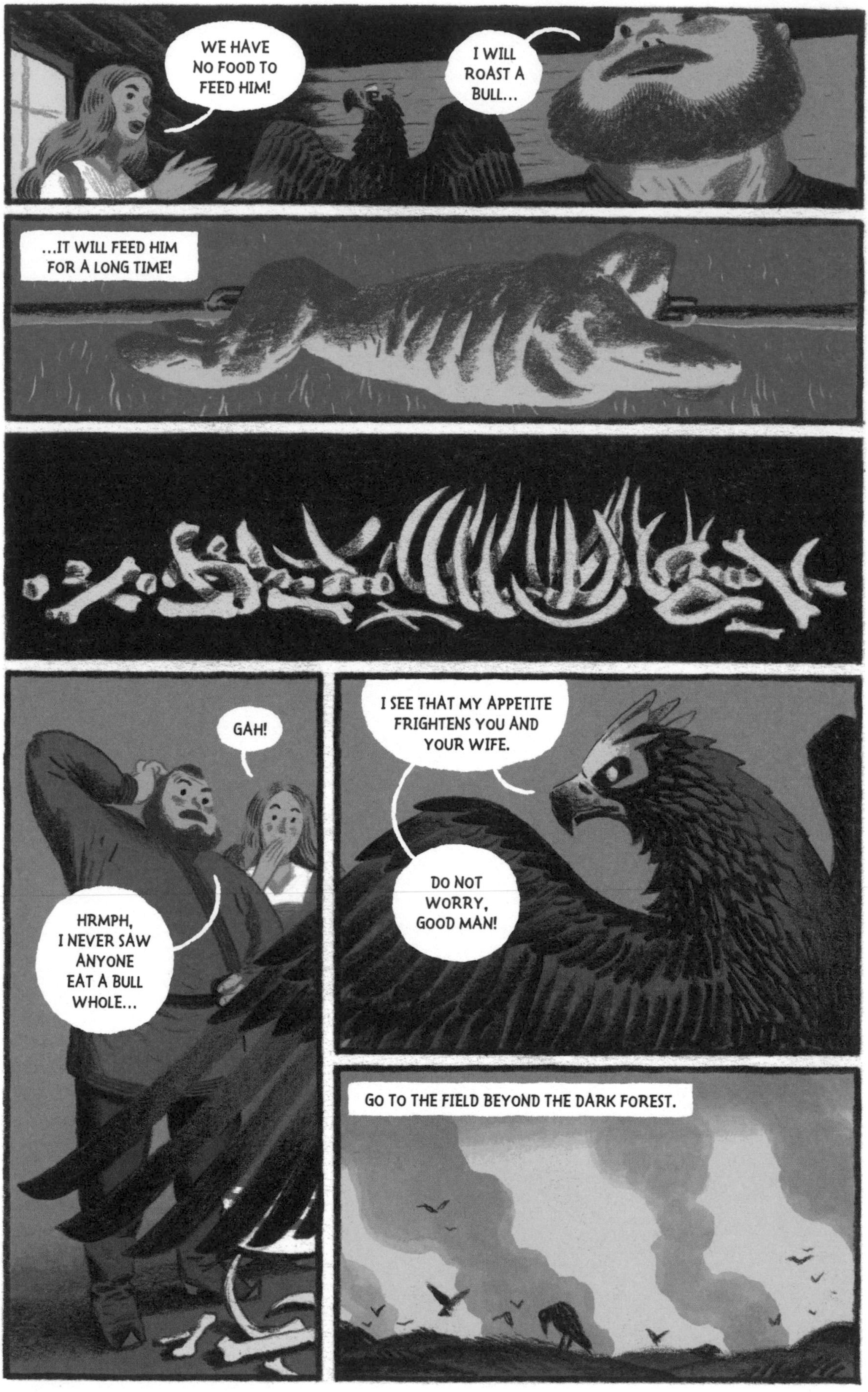
WE HAVE NO FOOD TO FEED HIM!
I WILL ROAST A BULL...
...IT WILL FEED HIM FOR A LONG TIME!
GAH!
HRMPH, I NEVER SAW ANYONE EAT A BULL WHOLE...
I SEE THAT MY APPETITE FRIGHTENS YOU AND YOUR WIFE.
DO NOT WORRY, GOOD MAN!
GO TO THE FIELD BEYOND THE DARK FOREST.

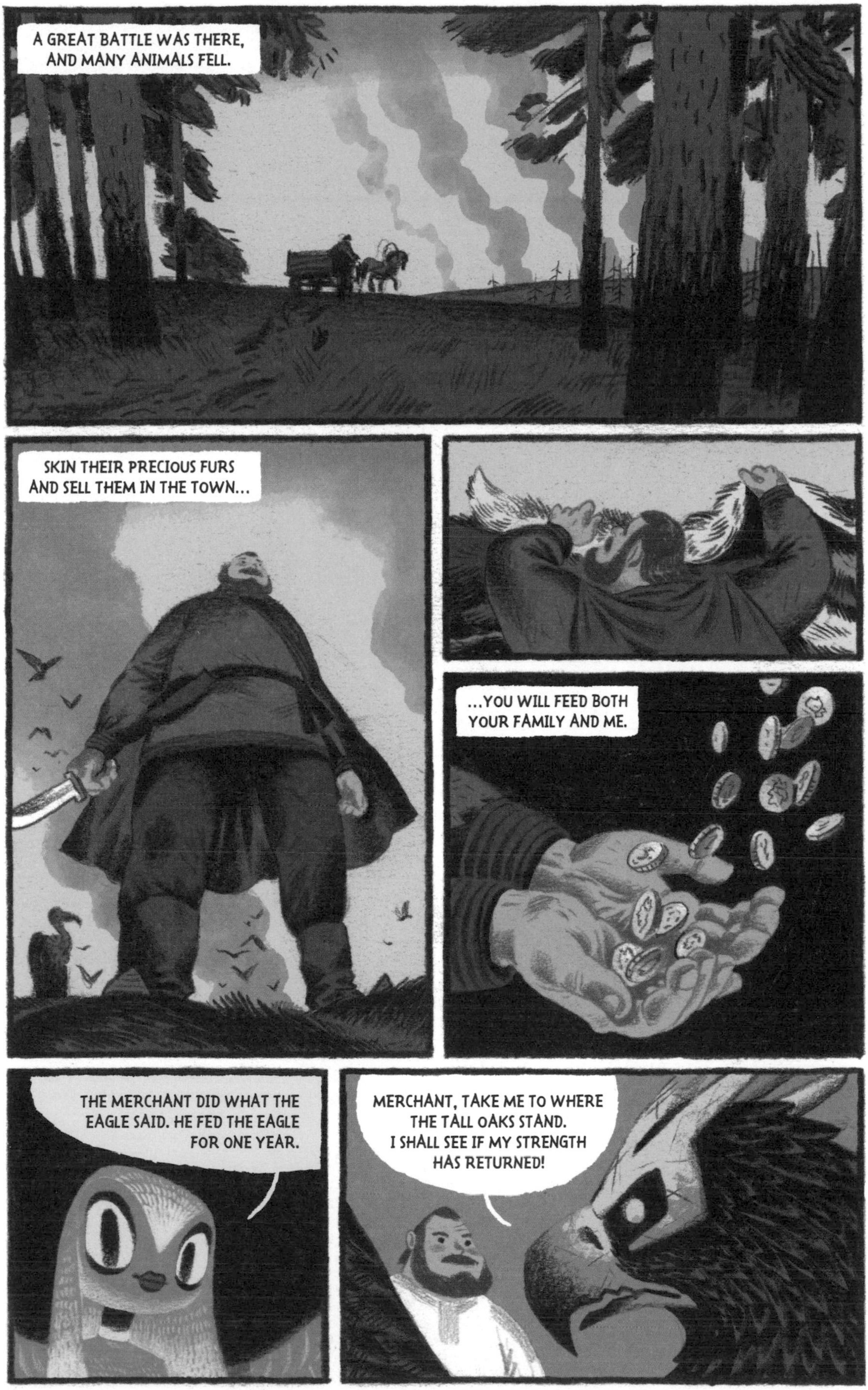
A GREAT BATTLE WAS THERE, AND MANY ANIMALS FELL.
SKIN THEIR PRECIOUS FURS AND SELL THEM IN THE TOWN...
...YOU WILL FEED BOTH YOUR FAMILY AND ME.
THE MERCHANT DID WHAT THE EAGLE SAID. HE FED THE EAGLE FOR ONE YEAR.
MERCHANT, TAKE ME TO WHERE THE TALL OAKS STAND. I SHALL SEE IF MY STRENGTH HAS RETURNED!

SOON THEY WERE THERE.

THE EAGLE FLEW HIGH INTO THE SKY...

HIS STRIKE SPLIT AN OLD OAK.

...AND PLUMMETED LIKE A STONE.

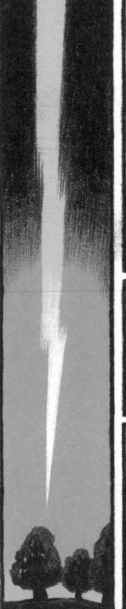

WHAT MIGHT YOU HAVE! I SEE YOU'VE RECOVERED.

NO, MERCHANT.

MY FULL MIGHT HAS NOT RETURNED. FEED ME FOR ANOTHER YEAR.

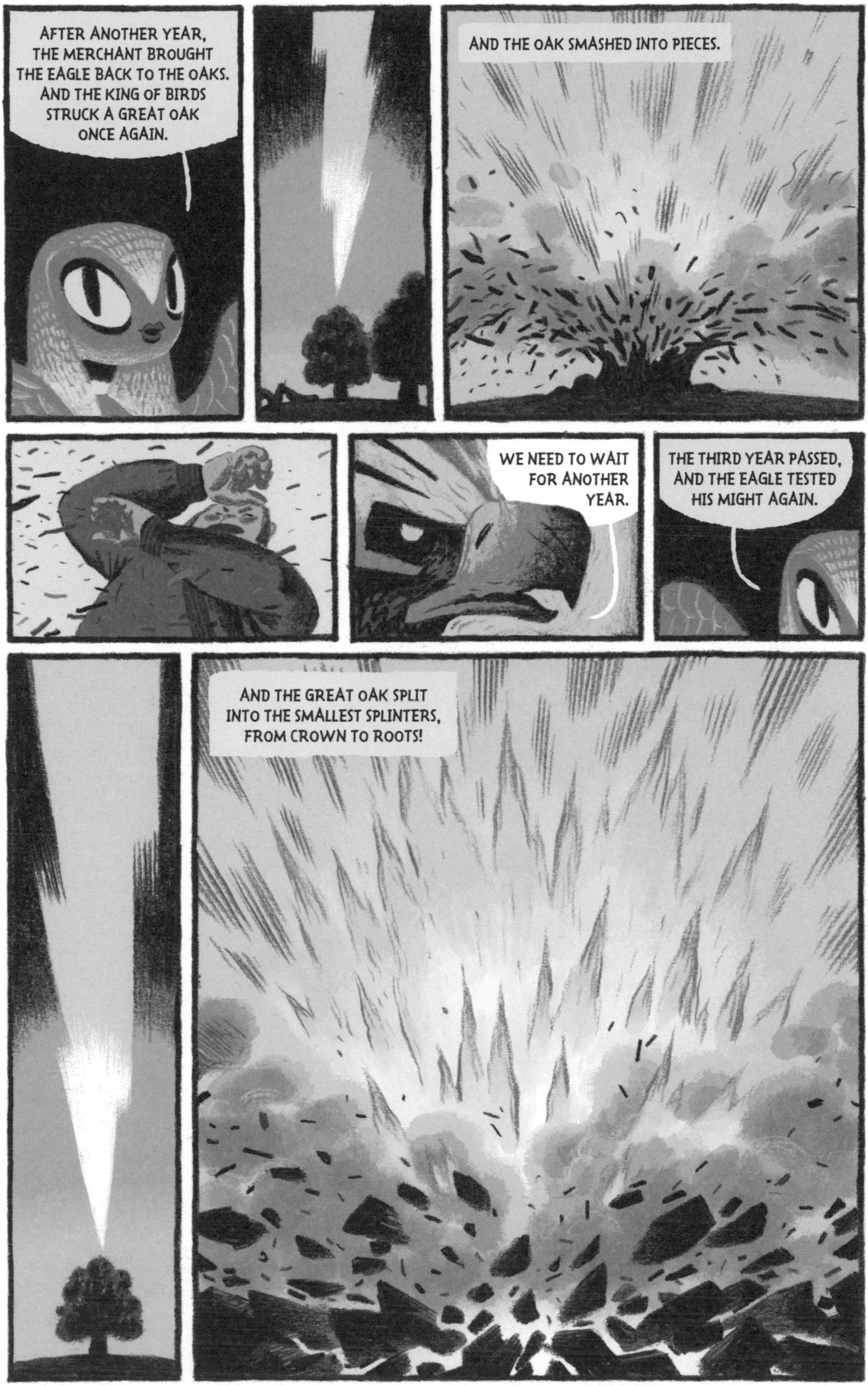
AFTER ANOTHER YEAR, THE MERCHANT BROUGHT THE EAGLE BACK TO THE OAKS. AND THE KING OF BIRDS STRUCK A GREAT OAK ONCE AGAIN.
AND THE OAK SMASHED INTO PIECES.
WE NEED TO WAIT FOR ANOTHER YEAR.
THE THIRD YEAR PASSED, AND THE EAGLE TESTED HIS MIGHT AGAIN.
AND THE GREAT OAK SPLIT INTO THE SMALLEST SPLINTERS, FROM CROWN TO ROOTS!

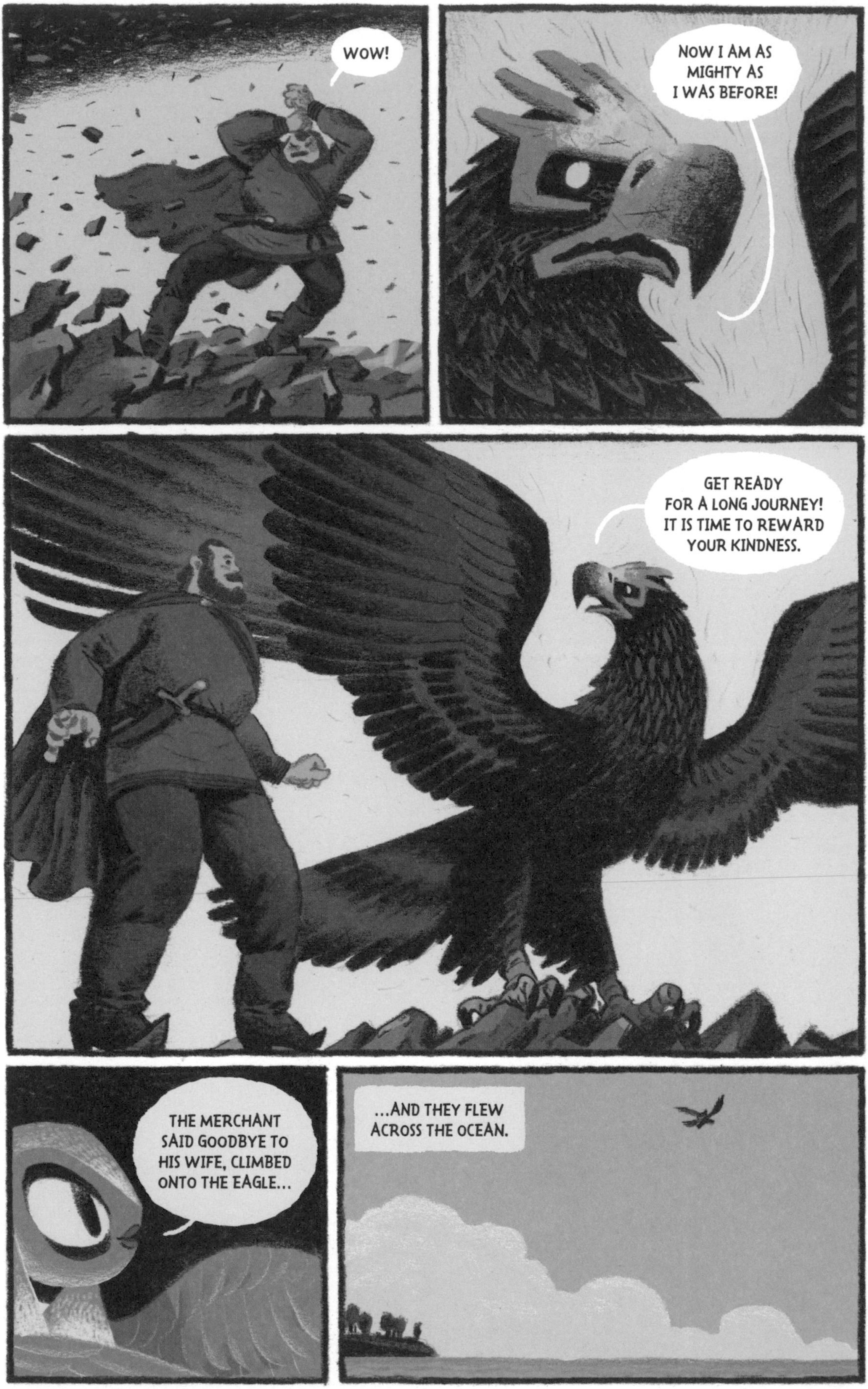
WOW!
NOW I AM AS MIGHTY AS I WAS BEFORE!
GET READY FOR A LONG JOURNEY! IT IS TIME TO REWARD YOUR KINDNESS.
THE MERCHANT SAID GOODBYE TO HIS WIFE, CLIMBED ONTO THE EAGLE...
...AND THEY FLEW ACROSS THE OCEAN.

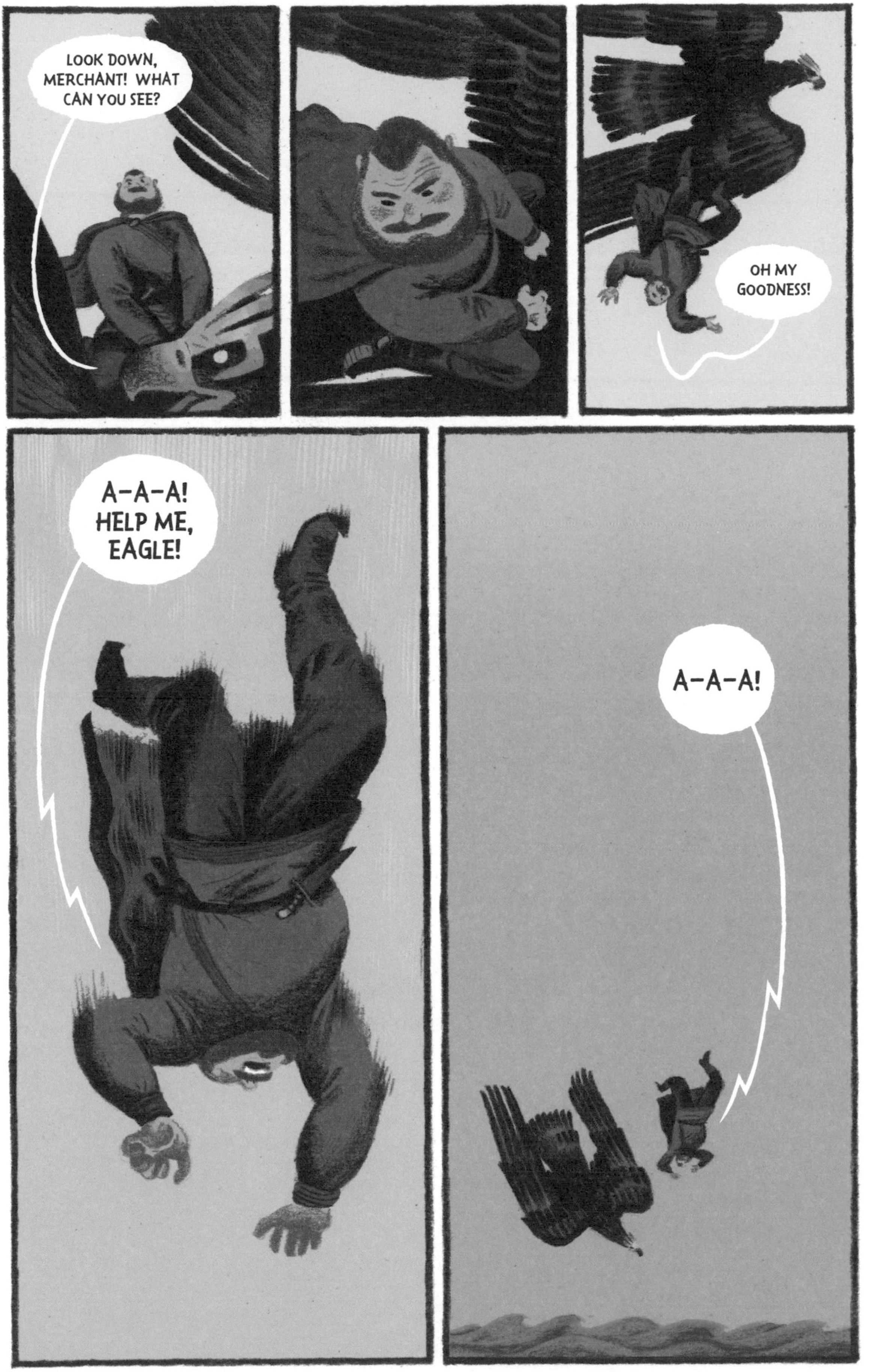
LOOK DOWN, MERCHANT! WHAT CAN YOU SEE?
OH MY GOODNESS!
A-A-A! HELP ME, EAGLE!
A-A-A!

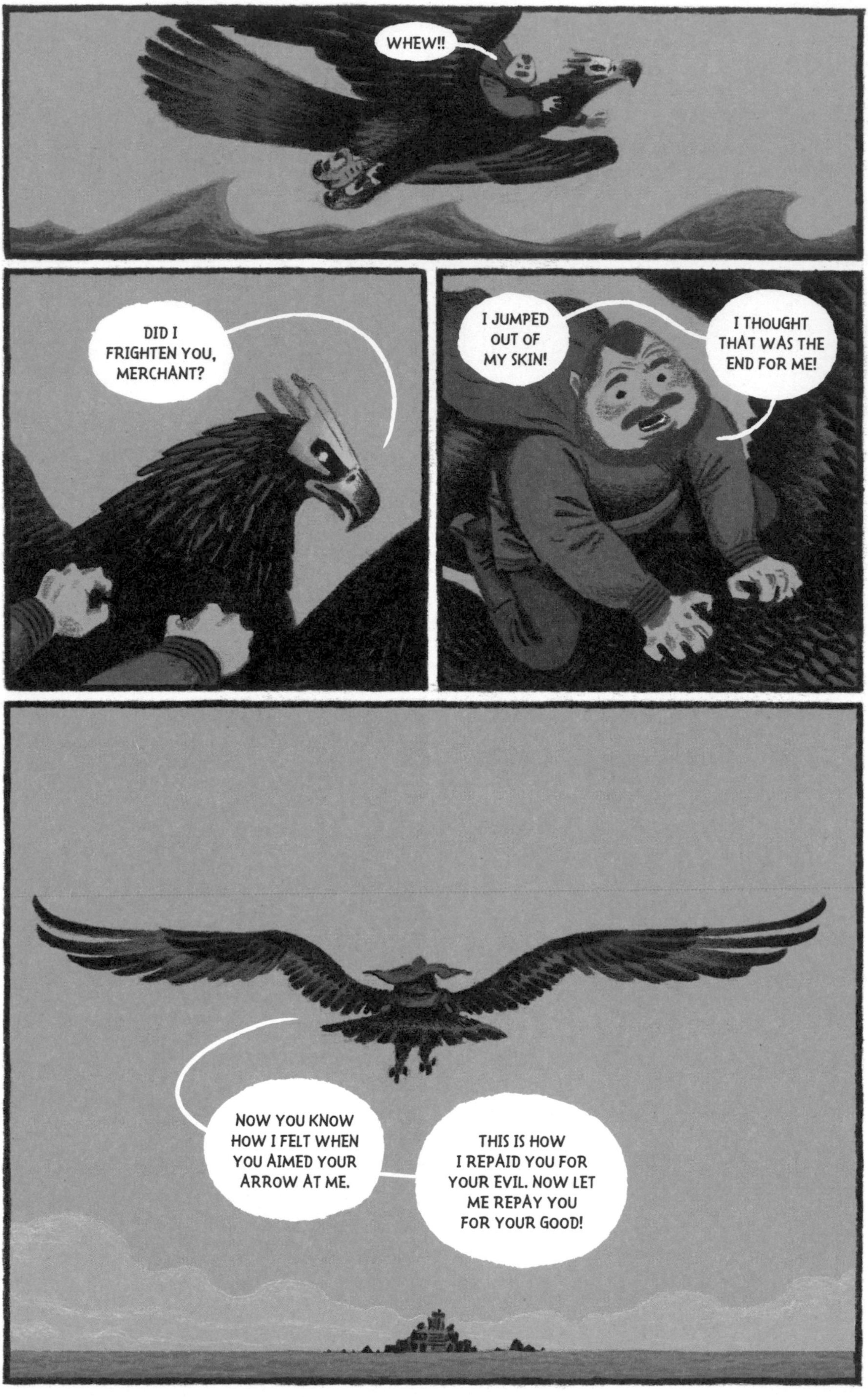
WHEW!!
DID I FRIGHTEN YOU, MERCHANT?
I JUMPED OUT OF MY SKIN!
I THOUGHT THAT WAS THE END FOR ME!
NOW YOU KNOW HOW I FELT WHEN YOU AIMED YOUR ARROW AT ME.
THIS IS HOW I REPAID YOU FOR YOUR EVIL. NOW LET ME REPAY YOU FOR YOUR GOOD!

THE COPPER REALM

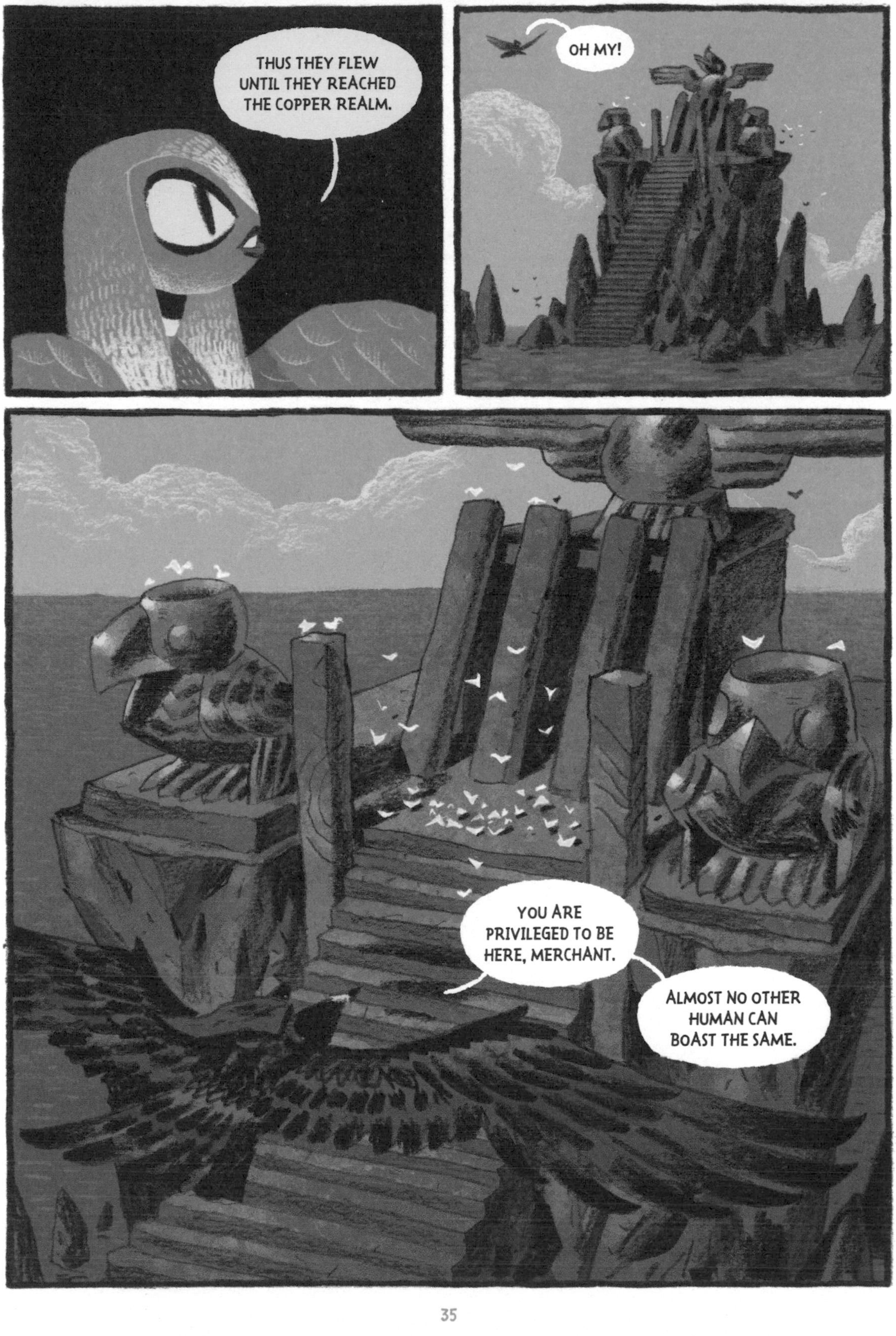
THUS THEY FLEW UNTIL THEY REACHED THE COPPER REALM.
OH MY!
YOU ARE PRIVILEGED TO BE HERE, MERCHANT.
ALMOST NO OTHER HUMAN CAN BOAST THE SAME.

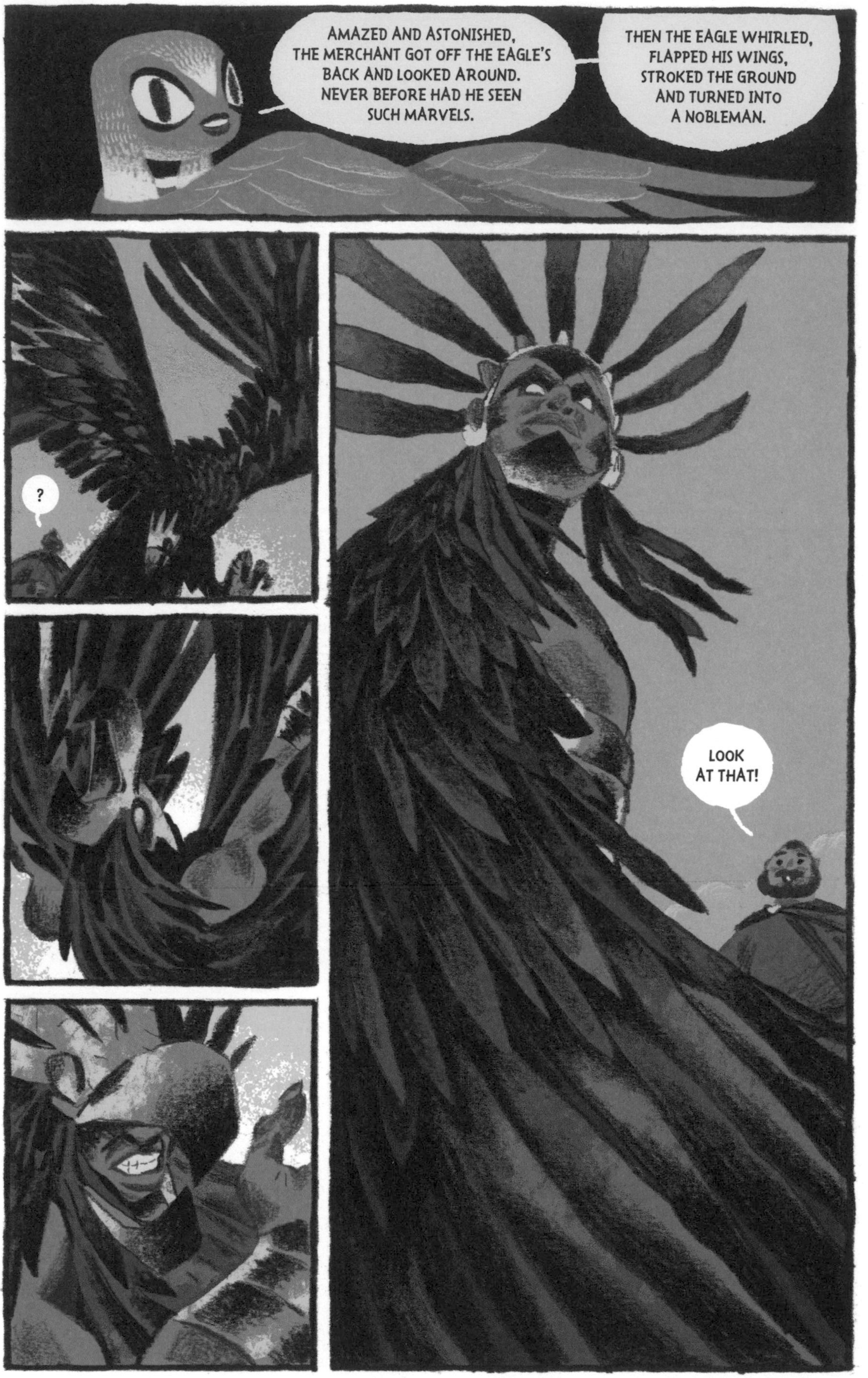
AMAZED AND ASTONISHED, THE MERCHANT GOT OFF THE EAGLE'S BACK AND LOOKED AROUND. NEVER BEFORE HAD HE SEEN SUCH MARVELS.
THEN THE EAGLE WHIRLED, FLAPPED HIS WINGS, STROKED THE GROUND AND TURNED INTO A NOBLEMAN.
?
LOOK AT THAT!

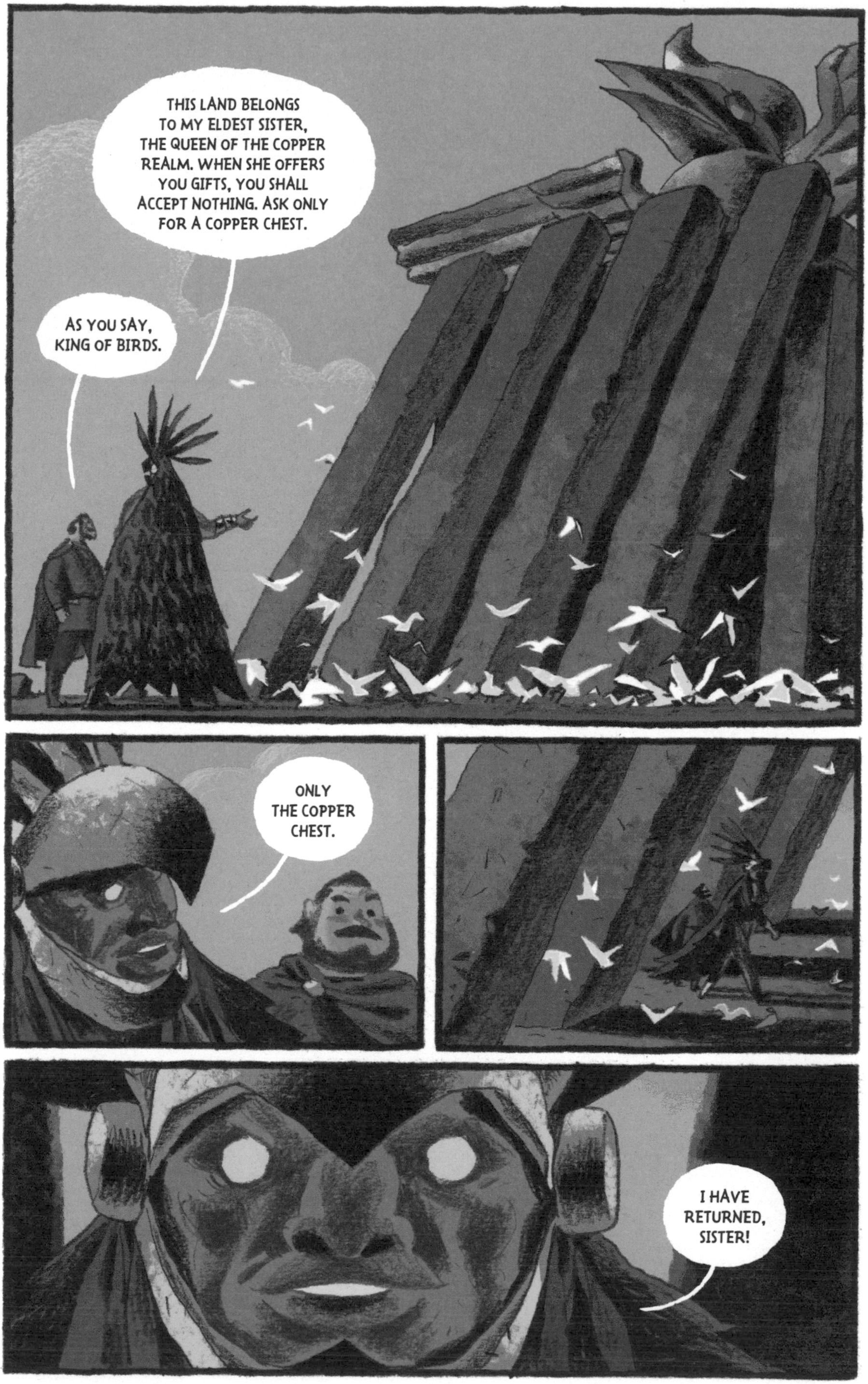
THIS LAND BELONGS TO MY ELDEST SISTER, THE QUEEN OF THE COPPER REALM. WHEN SHE OFFERS YOU GIFTS, YOU SHALL ACCEPT NOTHING. ASK ONLY FOR A COPPER CHEST.
AS YOU SAY, KING OF BIRDS.
ONLY THE COPPER CHEST.
I HAVE RETURNED, SISTER!

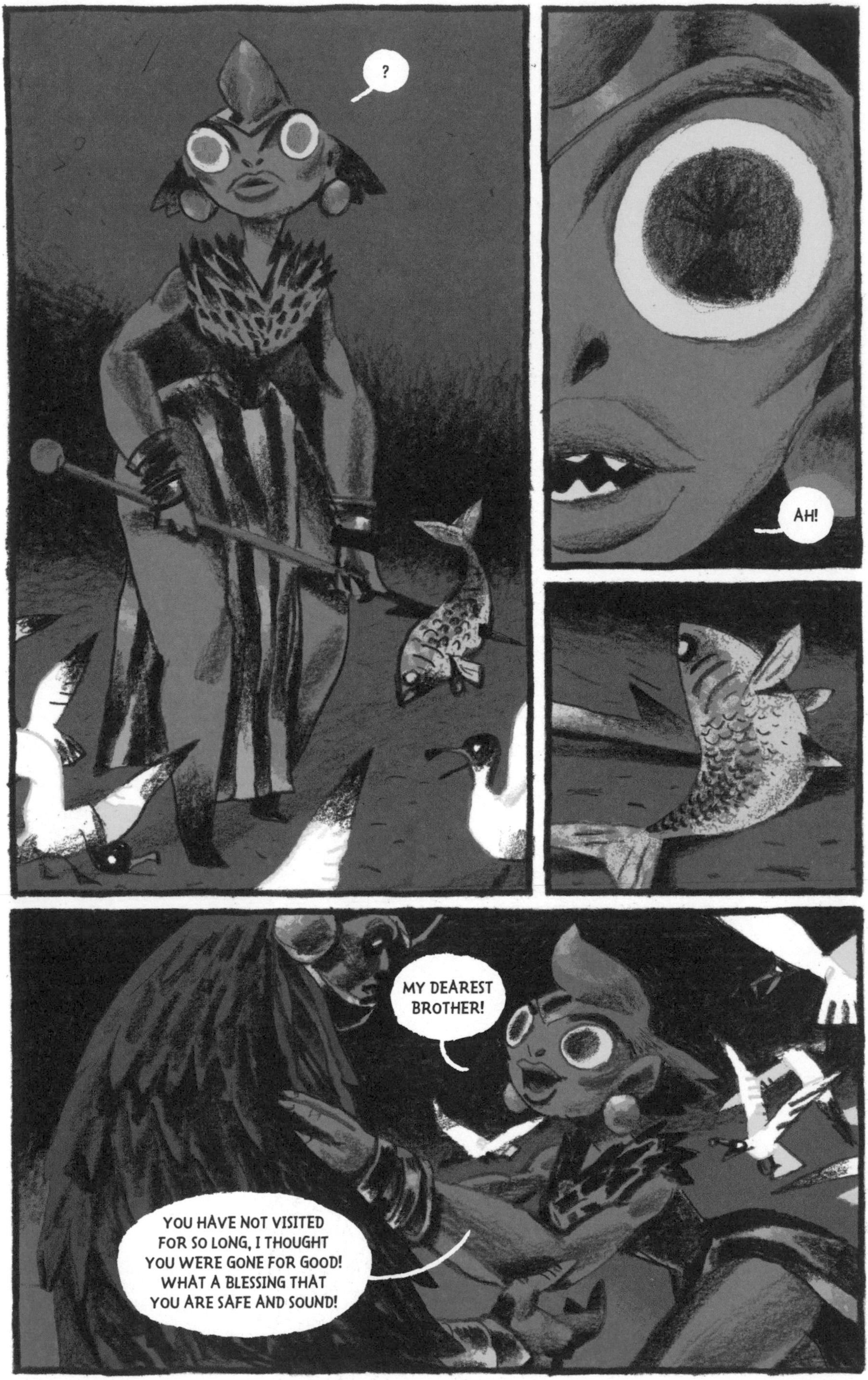
?
AH!
MY DEAREST BROTHER!
YOU HAVE NOT VISITED FOR SO LONG, I THOUGHT YOU WERE GONE FOR GOOD! WHAT A BLESSING THAT YOU ARE SAFE AND SOUND!

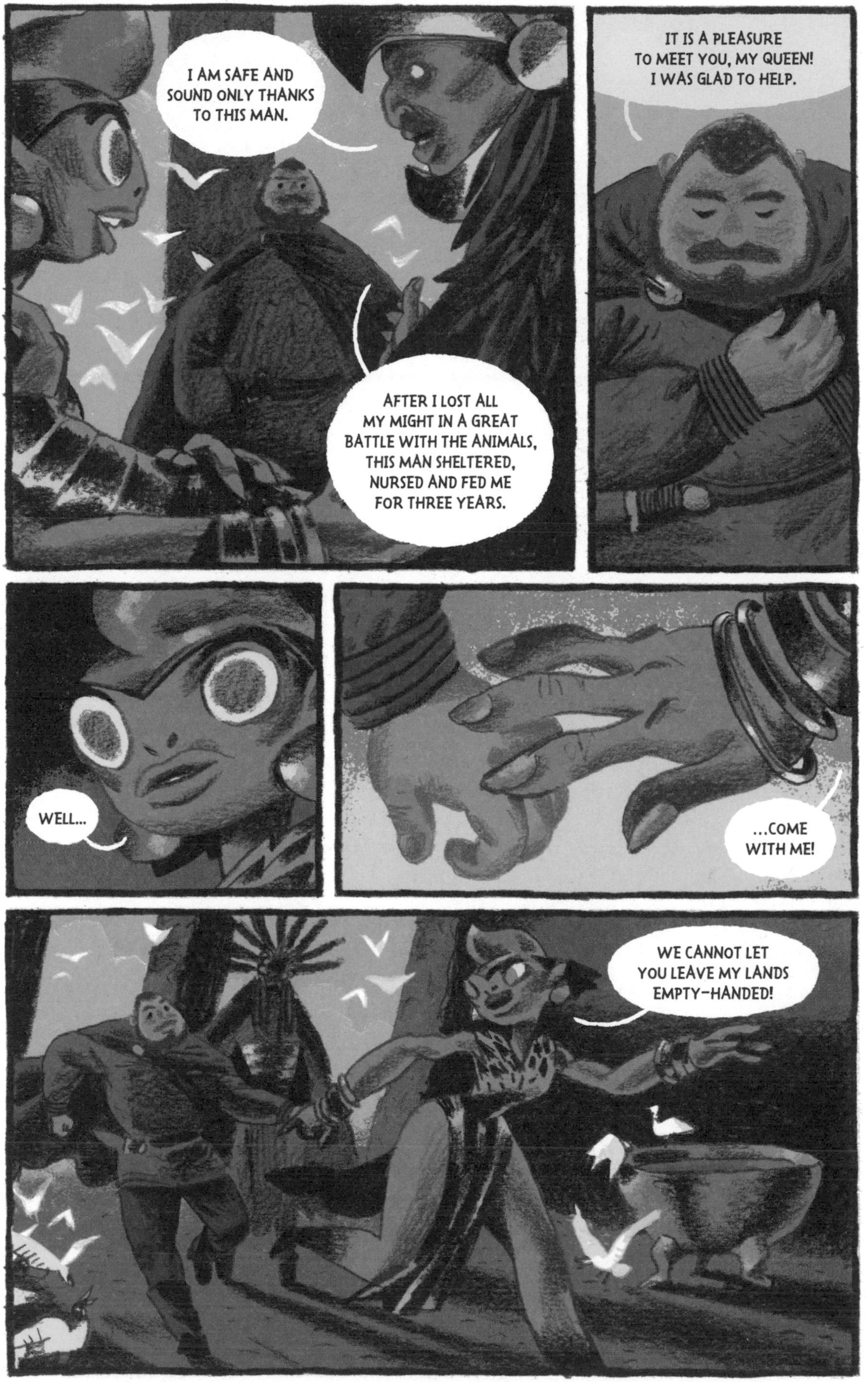
I AM SAFE AND SOUND ONLY THANKS TO THIS MAN.
AFTER I LOST ALL MY MIGHT IN A GREAT BATTLE WITH THE ANIMALS, THIS MAN SHELTERED, NURSED AND FED ME FOR THREE YEARS.
IT IS A PLEASURE TO MEET YOU, MY QUEEN! I WAS GLAD TO HELP.
WELL...
...COME WITH ME!
WE CANNOT LET YOU LEAVE MY LANDS EMPTY-HANDED!

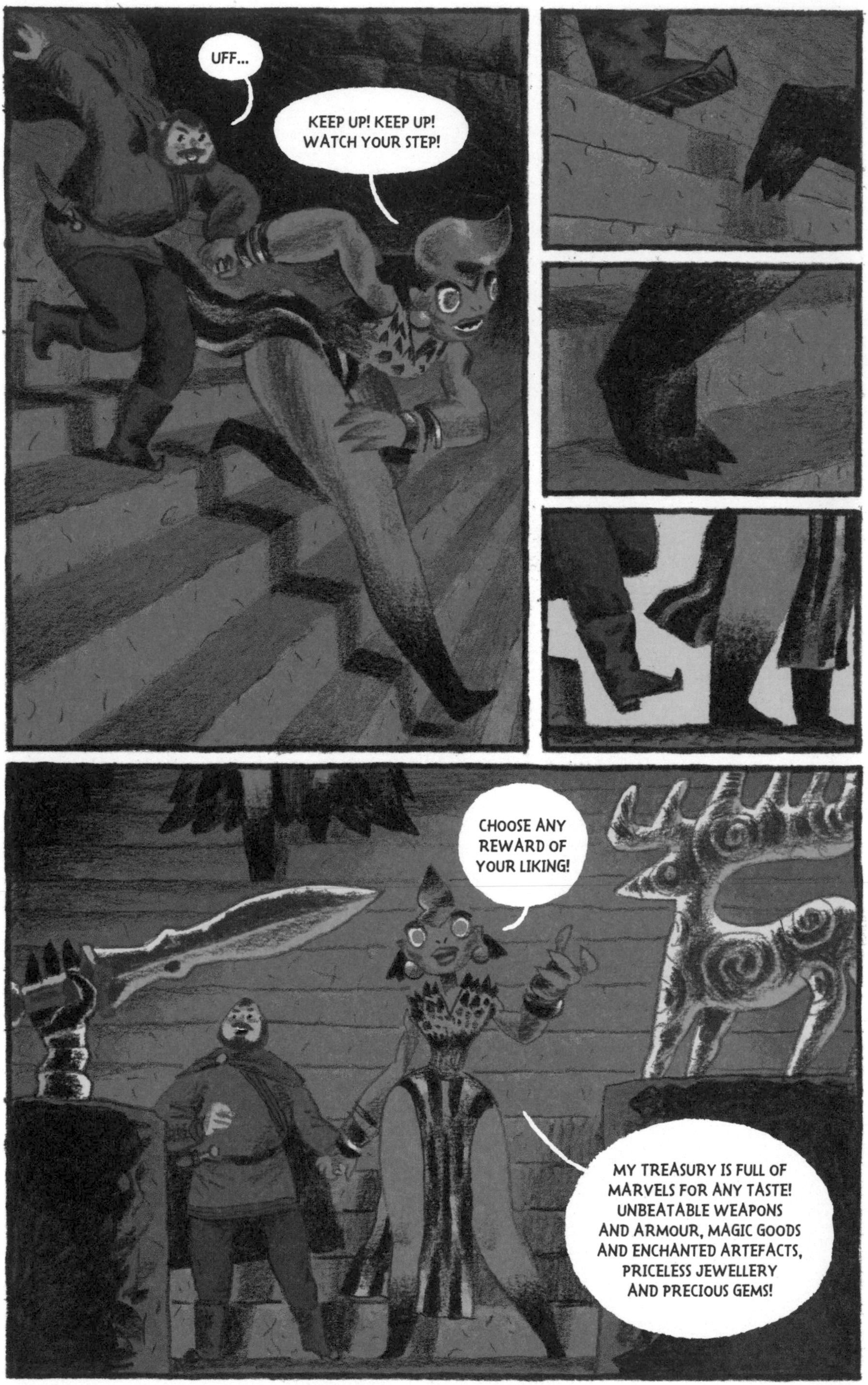
UFF...
KEEP UP! KEEP UP! WATCH YOUR STEP!
CHOOSE ANY REWARD OF YOUR LIKING!
MY TREASURY IS FULL OF MARVELS FOR ANY TASTE! UNBEATABLE WEAPONS AND ARMOUR, MAGIC GOODS AND ENCHANTED ARTEFACTS, PRICELESS JEWELLERY AND PRECIOUS GEMS!

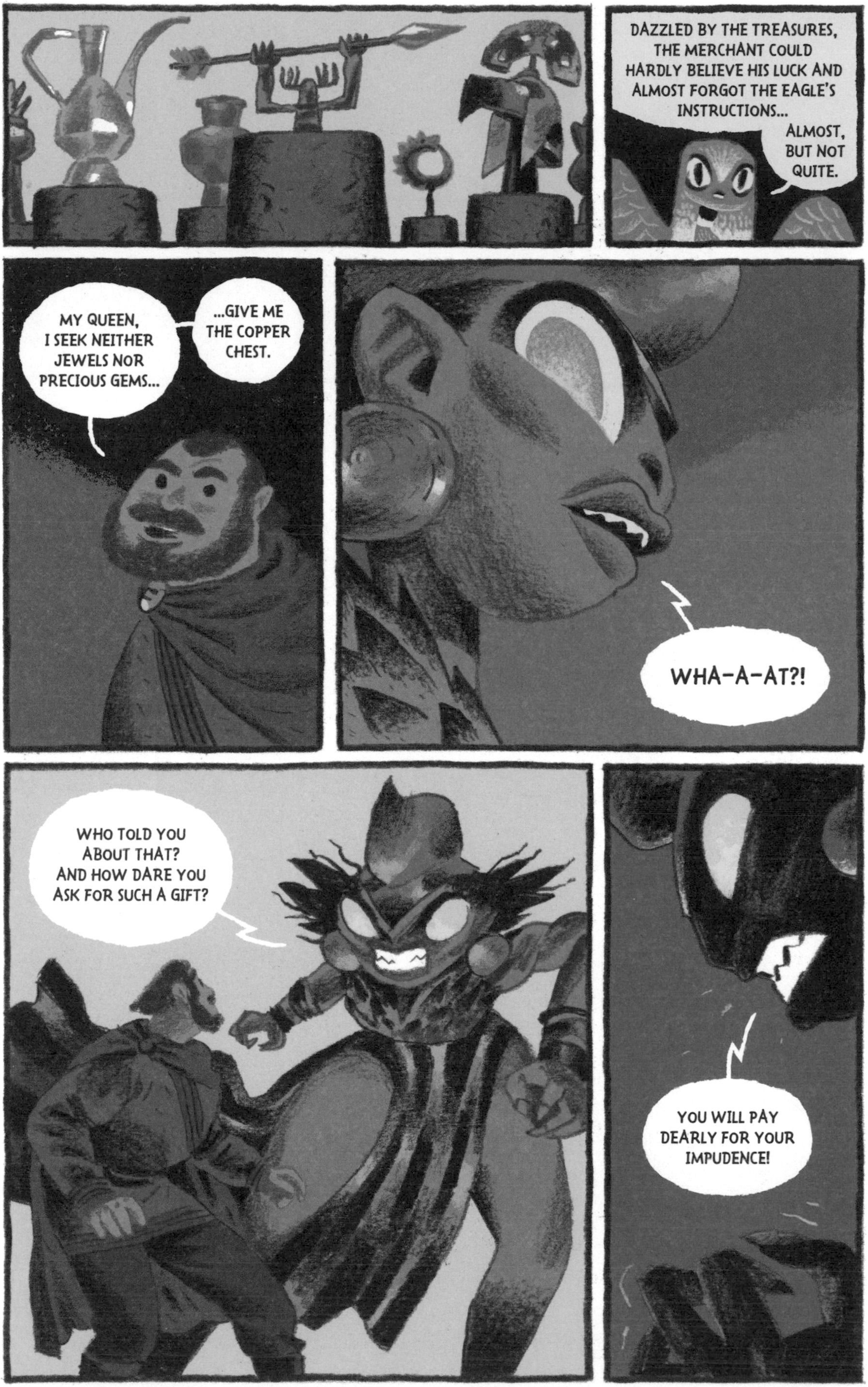

DAZZLED BY THE TREASURES, THE MERCHANT COULD HARDLY BELIEVE HIS LUCK AND ALMOST FORGOT THE EAGLE'S INSTRUCTIONS...
ALMOST, BUT NOT QUITE.
MY QUEEN, I SEEK NEITHER JEWELS NOR PRECIOUS GEMS...
...GIVE ME THE COPPER CHEST.
WHA-A-AT?!
WHO TOLD YOU ABOUT THAT? AND HOW DARE YOU ASK FOR SUCH A GIFT?
YOU WILL PAY DEARLY FOR YOUR IMPUDENCE!

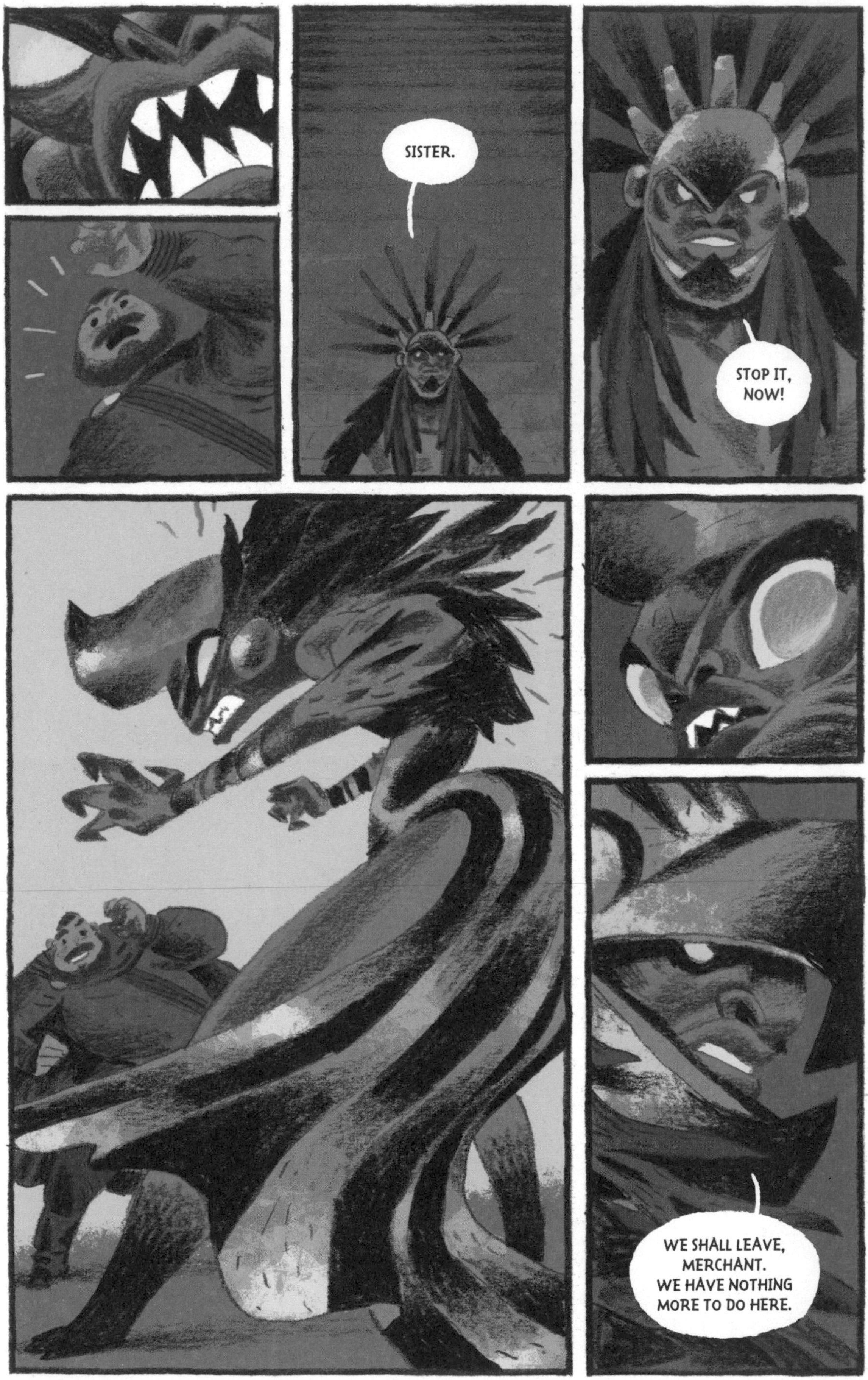
SISTER.
STOP IT, NOW!
WE SHALL LEAVE, MERCHANT. WE HAVE NOTHING MORE TO DO HERE.

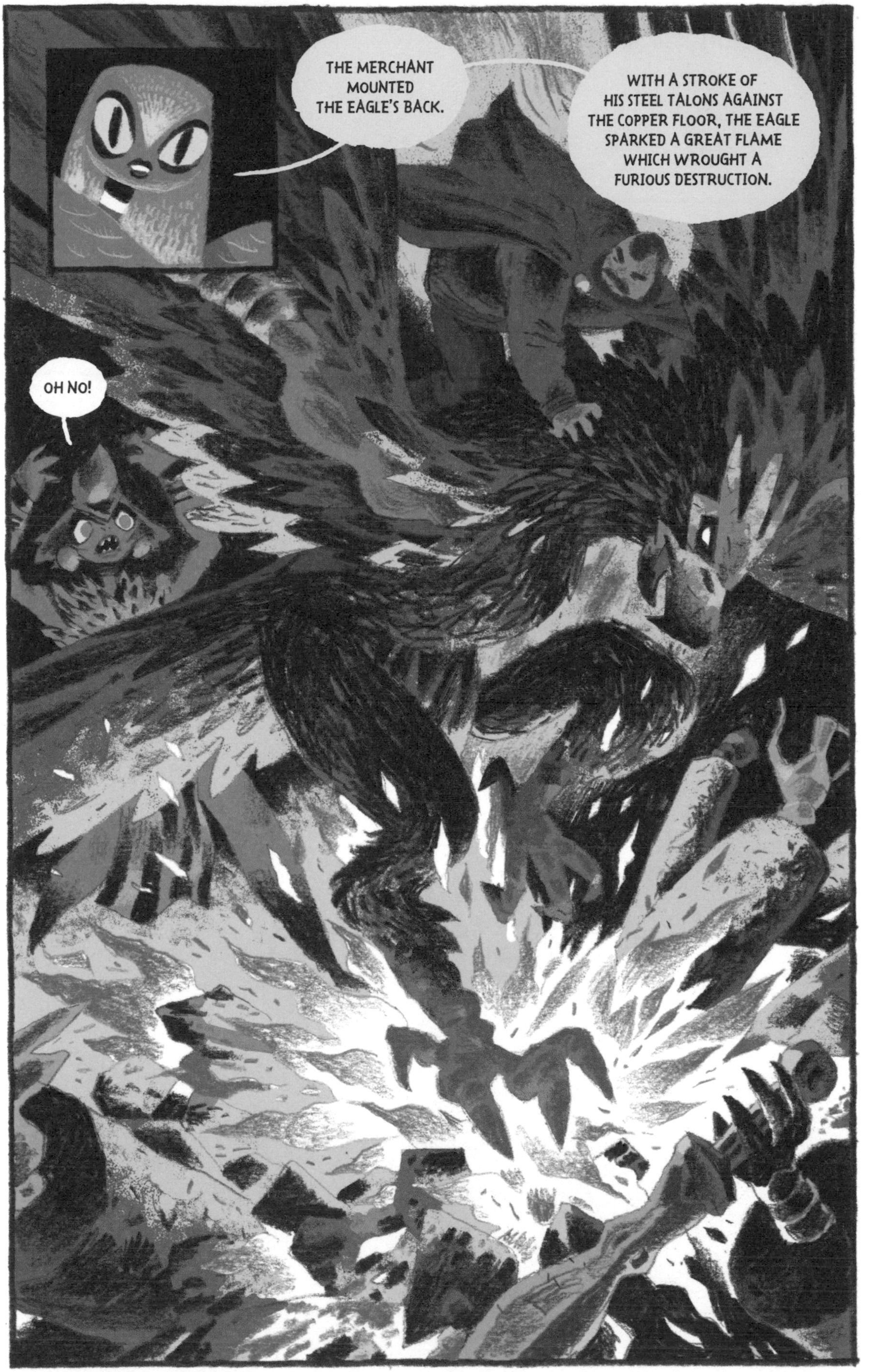
THE MERCHANT MOUNTED THE EAGLE'S BACK.
WITH A STROKE OF HIS STEEL TALONS AGAINST THE COPPER FLOOR, THE EAGLE SPARKED A GREAT FLAME WHICH WROUGHT A FURIOUS DESTRUCTION.
OH NO!

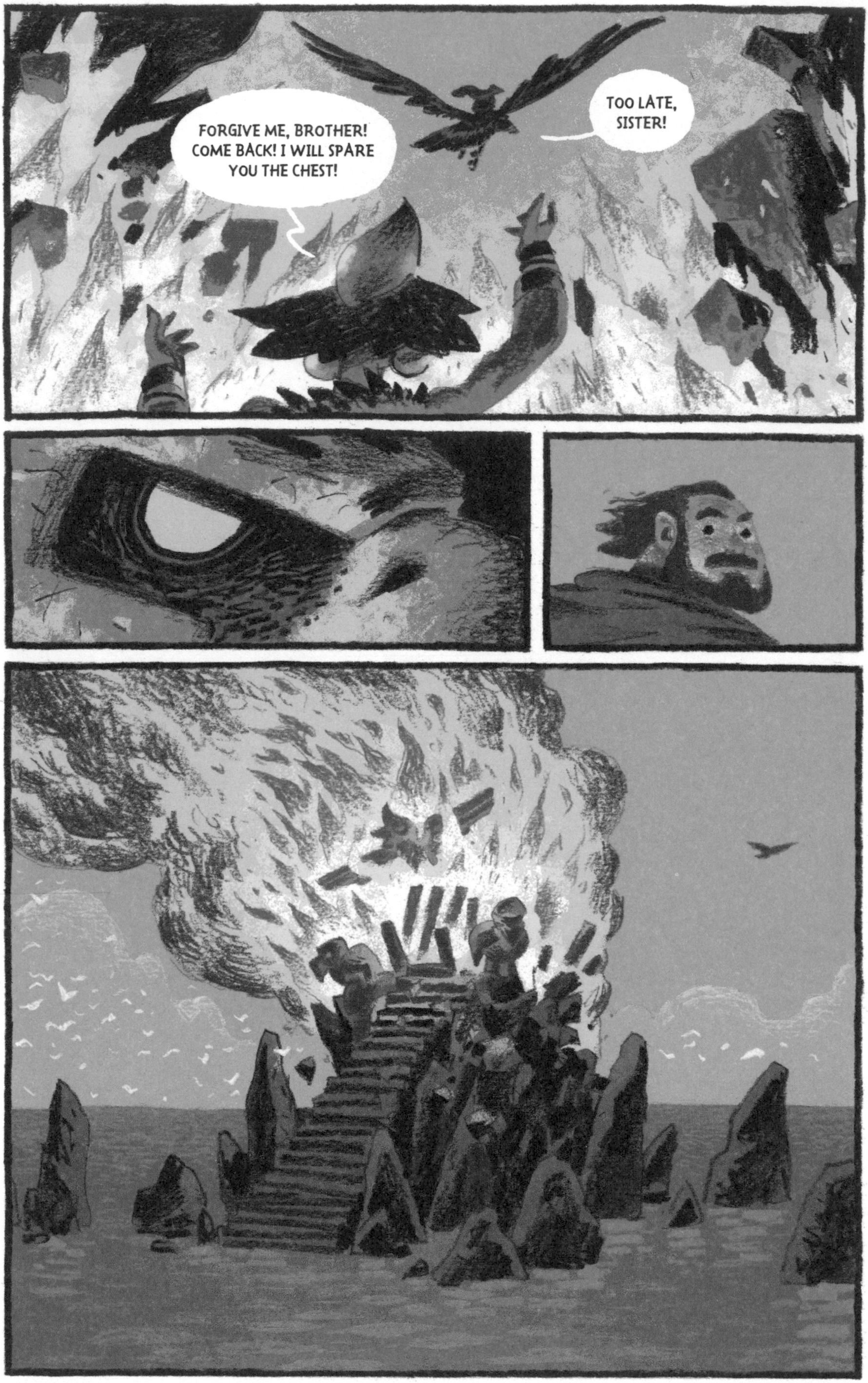
FORGIVE ME, BROTHER! COME BACK! I WILL SPARE YOU THE CHEST!
TOO LATE, SISTER!

THE SILVER REALM

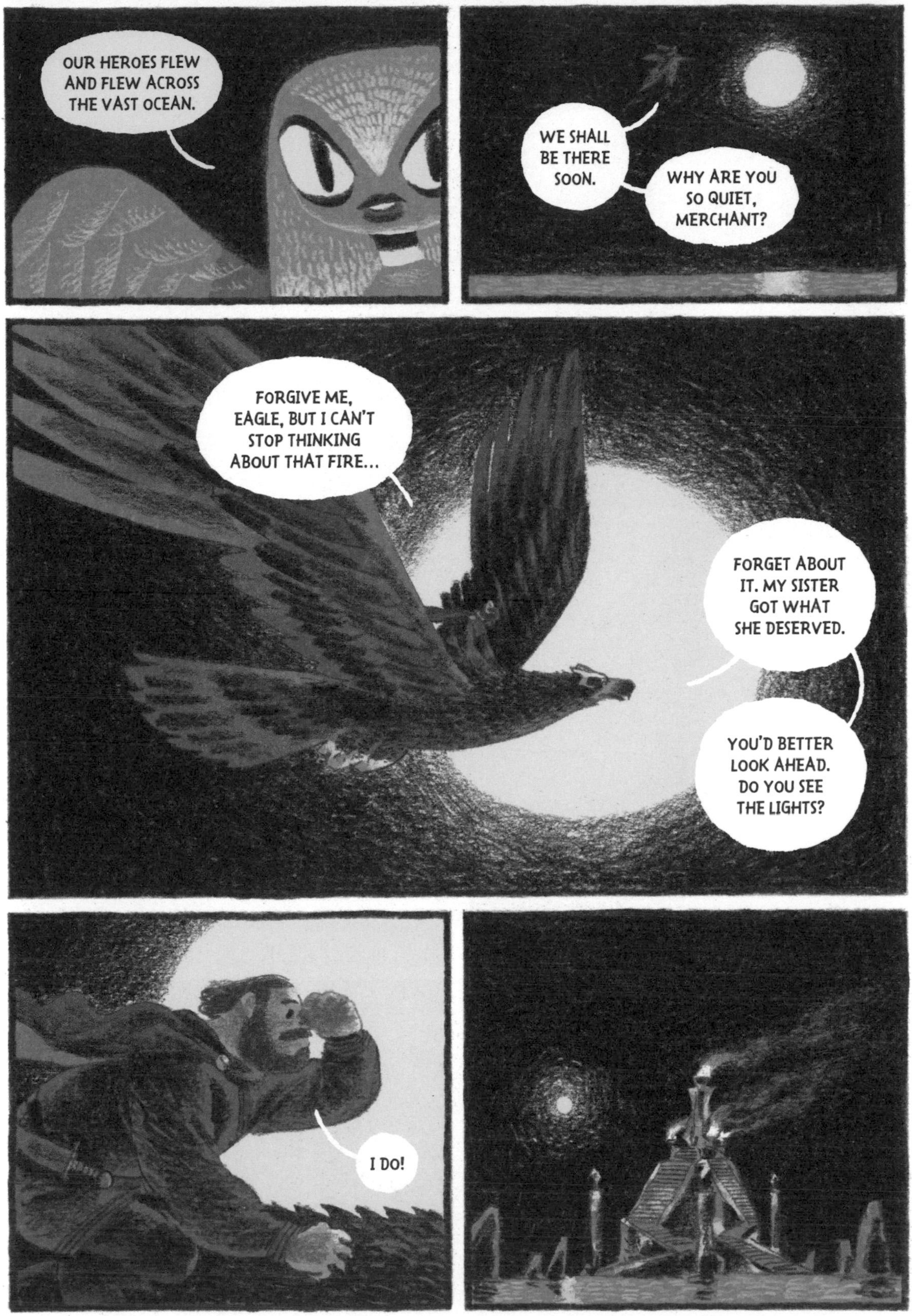
OUR HEROES FLEW AND FLEW ACROSS THE VAST OCEAN.
WE SHALL BE THERE SOON.
WHY ARE YOU SO QUIET, MERCHANT?
FORGIVE ME, EAGLE, BUT I CAN'T STOP THINKING ABOUT THAT FIRE...
FORGET ABOUT IT. MY SISTER GOT WHAT SHE DESERVED.
YOU'D BETTER LOOK AHEAD. DO YOU SEE THE LIGHTS?
I DO!

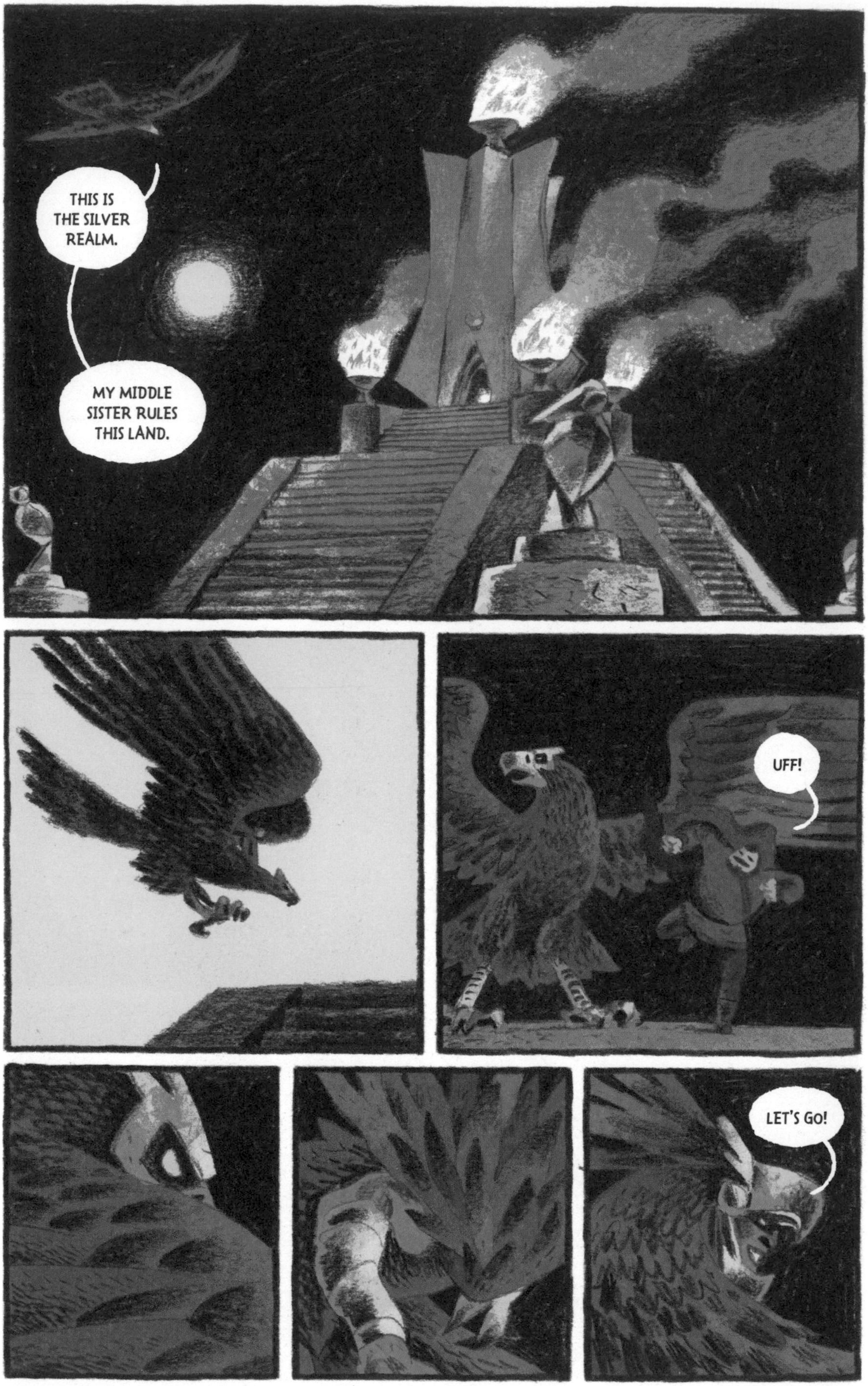
THIS IS THE SILVER REALM.
MY MIDDLE SISTER RULES THIS LAND.
UFF!
LET'S GO!

WILL SHE PERISH BECAUSE OF ME JUST LIKE HER SISTER?

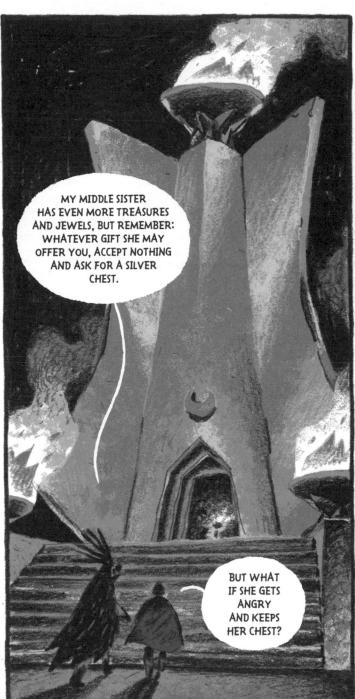

MY MIDDLE SISTER HAS EVEN MORE TREASURES AND JEWELS, BUT REMEMBER: WHATEVER GIFT SHE MAY OFFER YOU, ACCEPT NOTHING AND ASK FOR A SILVER CHEST.

BUT WHAT IF SHE GETS ANGRY AND KEEPS HER CHEST?

IT IS NO CONCERN OF YOURS, MERCHANT.

MARK THIS WELL: TAKE NOTHING BUT THE SILVER CHEST.

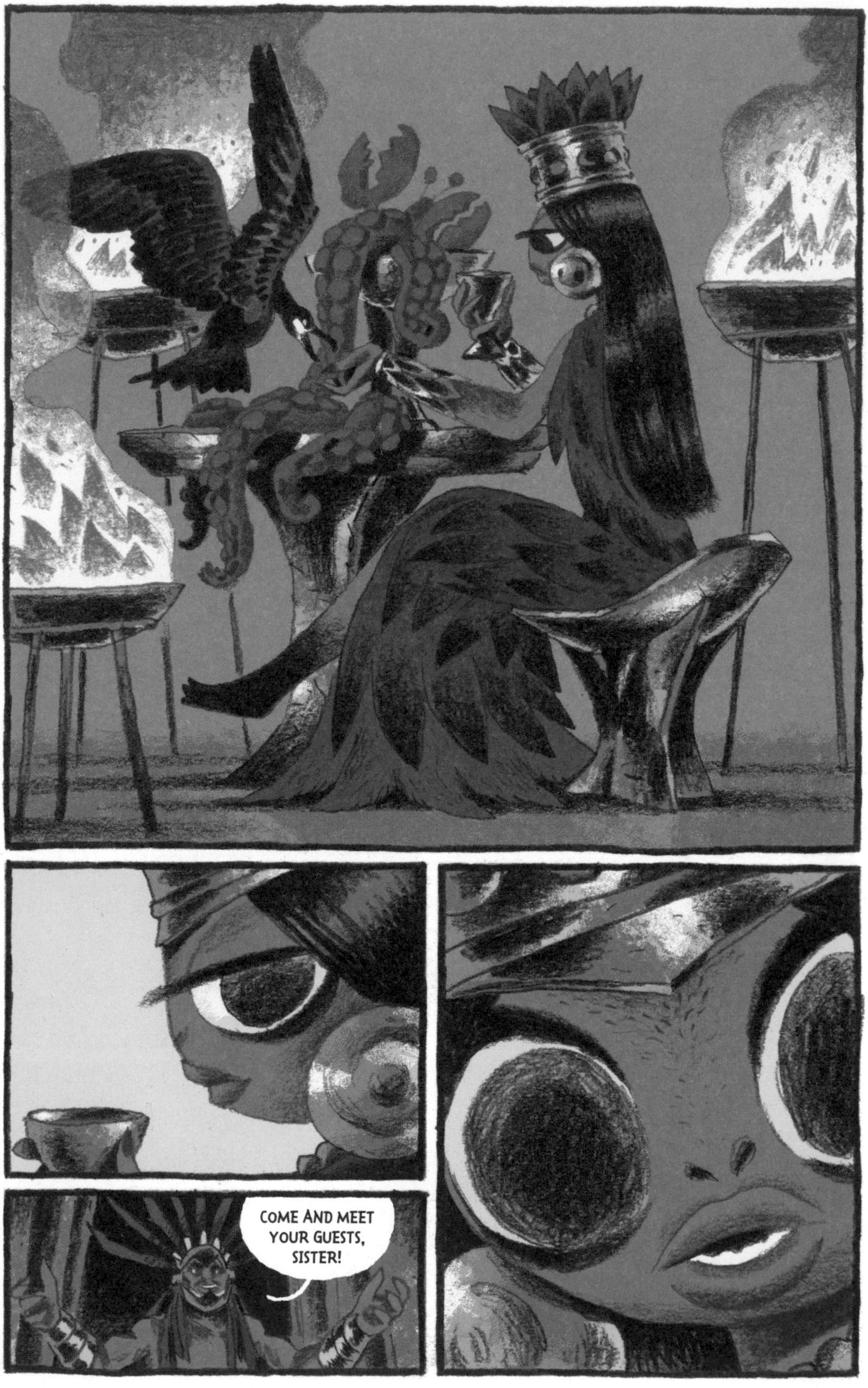
COME AND MEET YOUR GUESTS, SISTER!

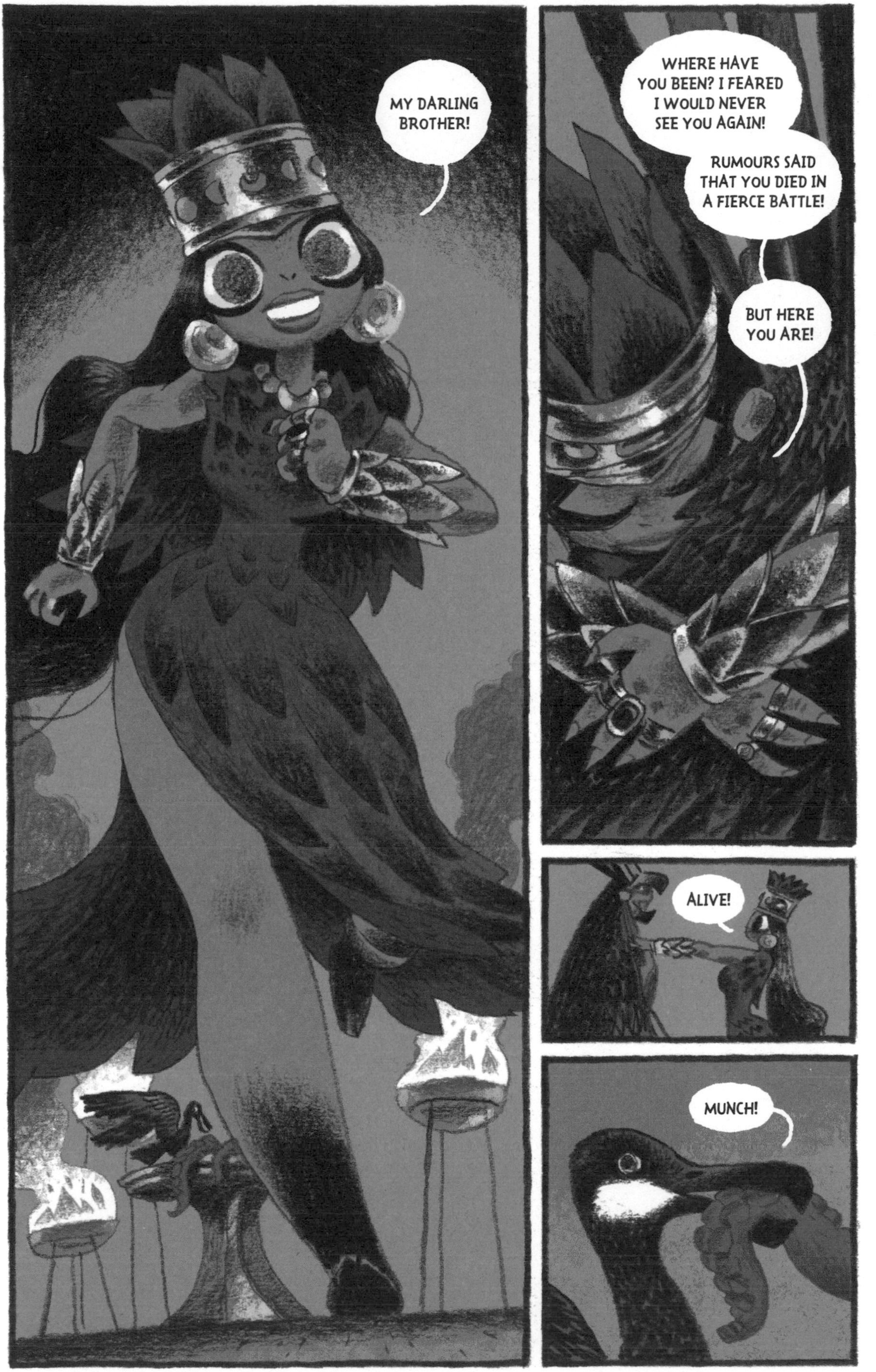
MY DARLING BROTHER!
WHERE HAVE YOU BEEN? I FEARED I WOULD NEVER SEE YOU AGAIN!
RUMOURS SAID THAT YOU DIED IN A FIERCE BATTLE!
BUT HERE YOU ARE!
ALIVE!
MUNCH!

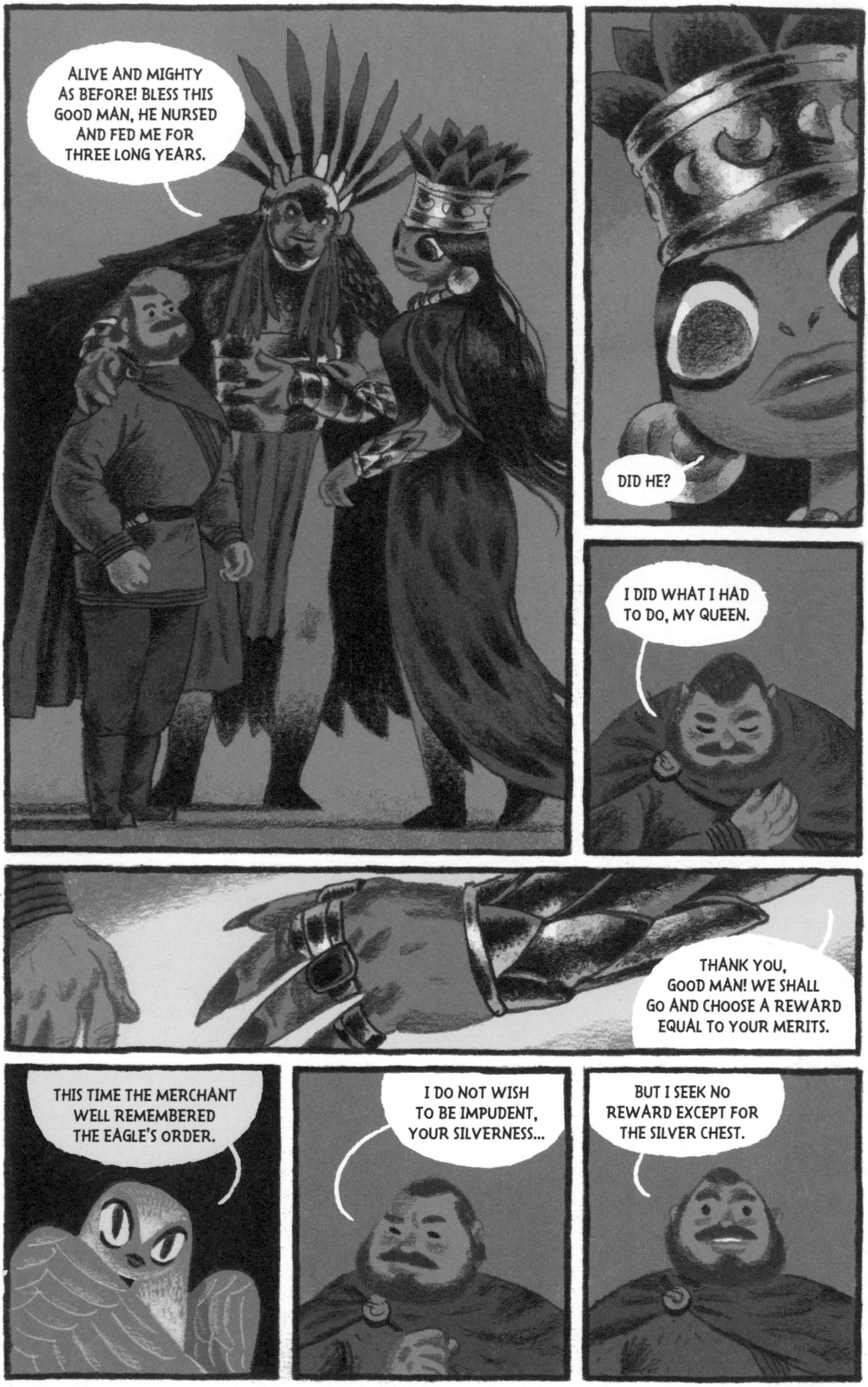
ALIVE AND MIGHTY AS BEFORE! BLESS THIS GOOD MAN, HE NURSED AND FED ME FOR THREE LONG YEARS.
DID HE?
I DID WHAT I HAD TO DO, MY QUEEN.
THANK YOU, GOOD MAN! WE SHALL GO AND CHOOSE A REWARD EQUAL TO YOUR MERITS.
THIS TIME THE MERCHANT WELL REMEMBERED THE EAGLE'S ORDER.
I DO NOT WISH TO BE IMPUDENT, YOUR SILVERNESS...
BUT I SEEK NO REWARD EXCEPT FOR THE SILVER CHEST.

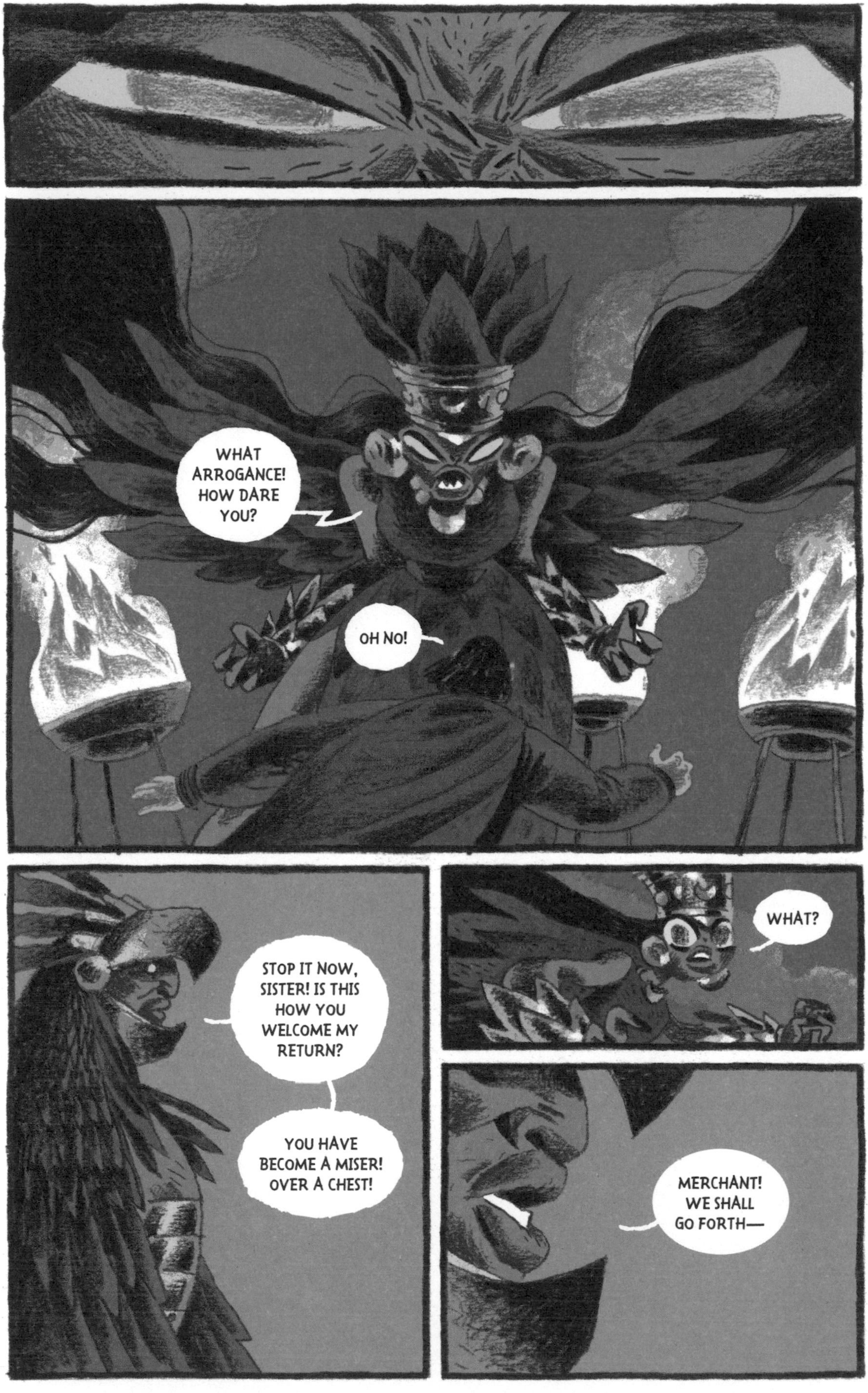
WHAT ARROGANCE! HOW DARE YOU?
OH NO!
STOP IT NOW, SISTER! IS THIS HOW YOU WELCOME MY RETURN?
YOU HAVE BECOME A MISER! OVER A CHEST!
WHAT?
MERCHANT! WE SHALL GO FORTH—

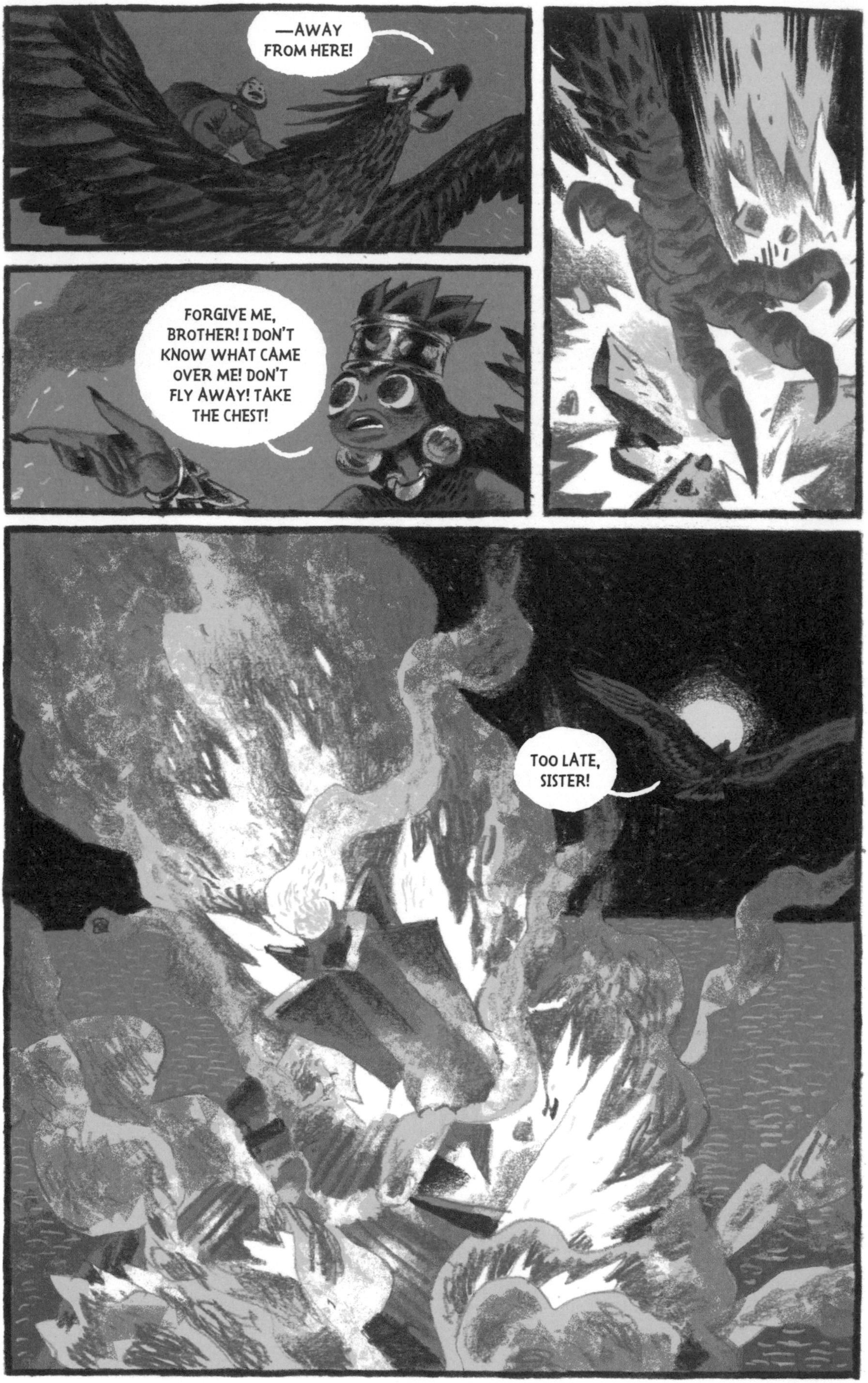
—AWAY FROM HERE!
FORGIVE ME, BROTHER! I DON'T KNOW WHAT CAME OVER ME! DON'T FLY AWAY! TAKE THE CHEST!
TOO LATE, SISTER!

THE GOLDEN REALM

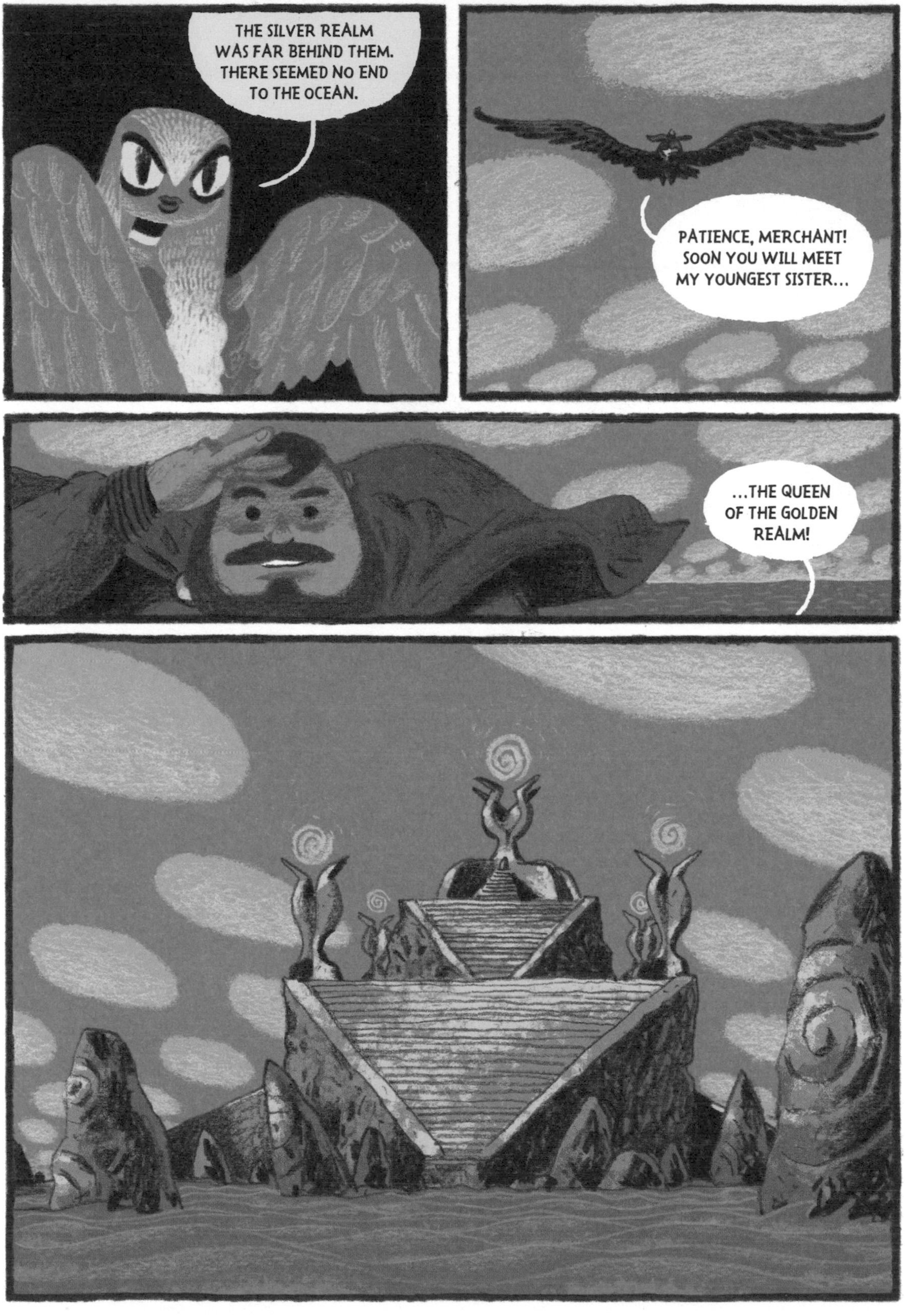
THE SILVER REALM WAS FAR BEHIND THEM. THERE SEEMED NO END TO THE OCEAN.
PATIENCE, MERCHANT! SOON YOU WILL MEET MY YOUNGEST SISTER...
...THE QUEEN OF THE GOLDEN REALM!

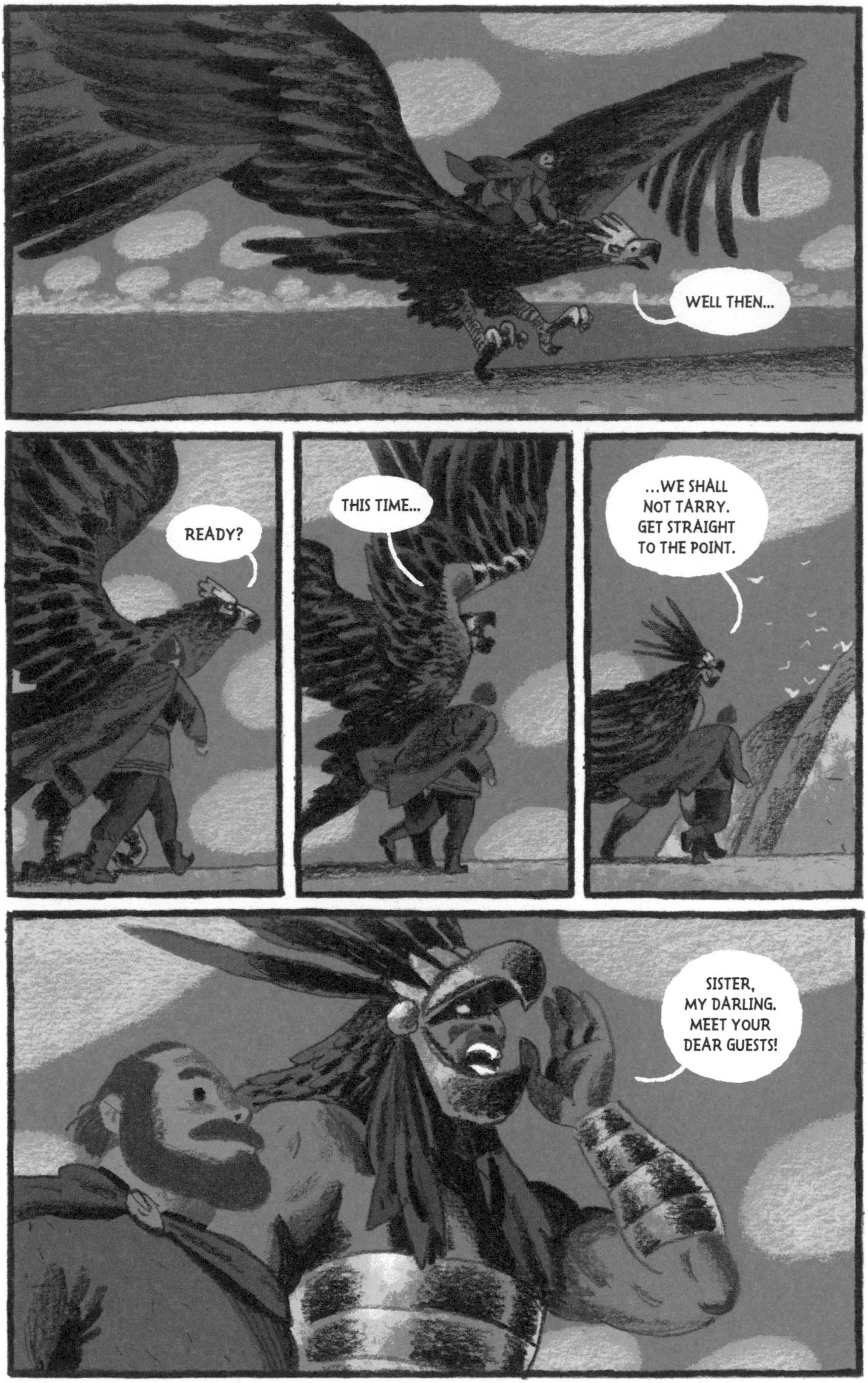
WELL THEN...
READY?
THIS TIME...
...WE SHALL NOT TARRY. GET STRAIGHT TO THE POINT.
SISTER, MY DARLING. MEET YOUR DEAR GUESTS!

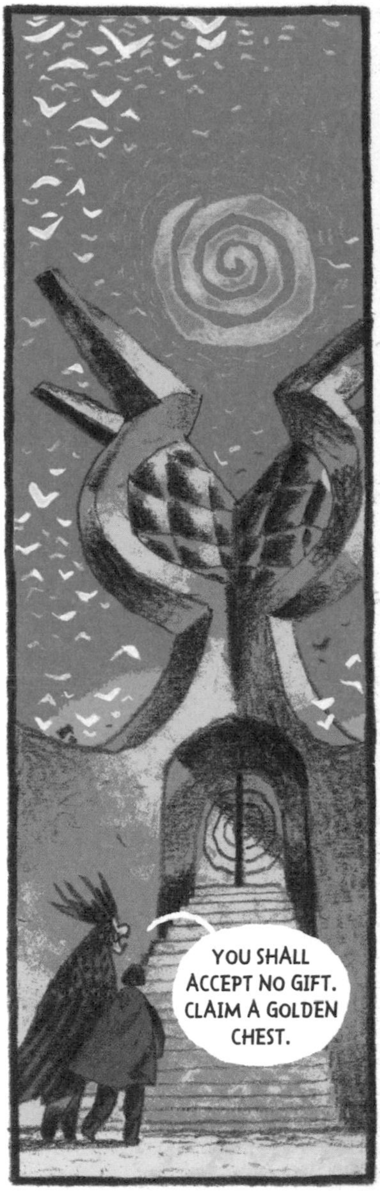
YOU SHALL ACCEPT NO GIFT. CLAIM A GOLDEN CHEST.

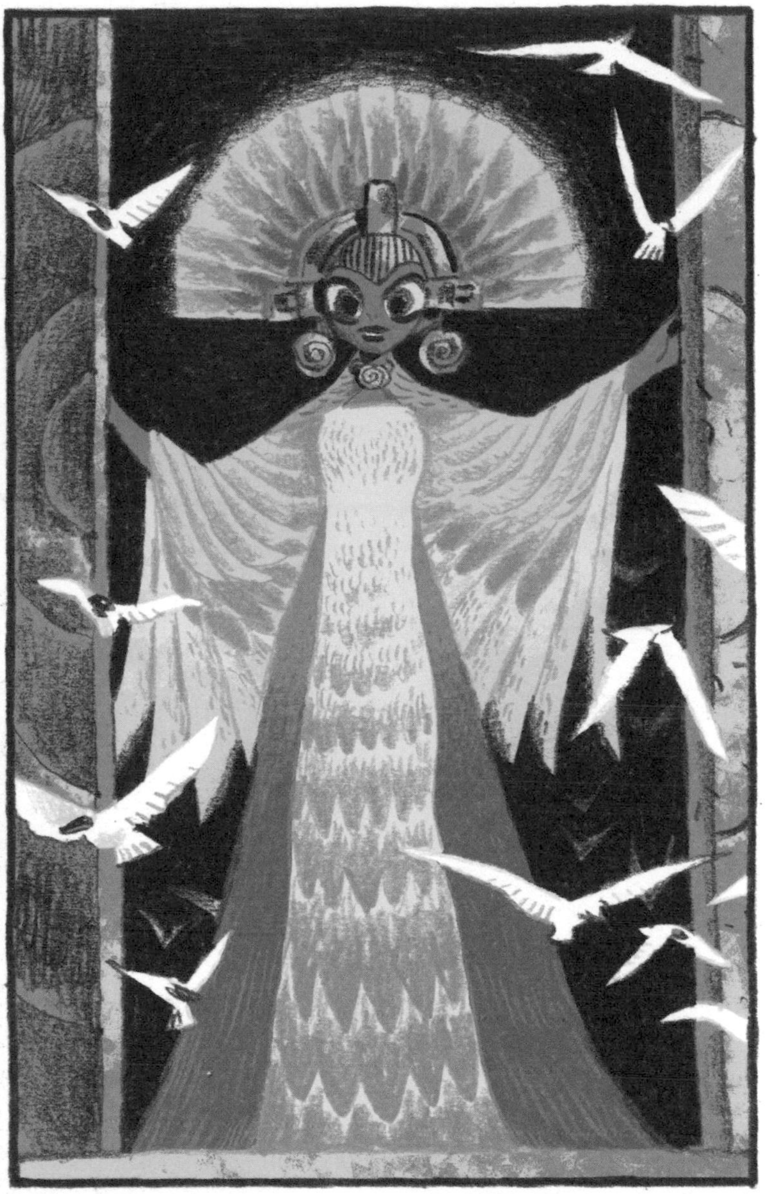

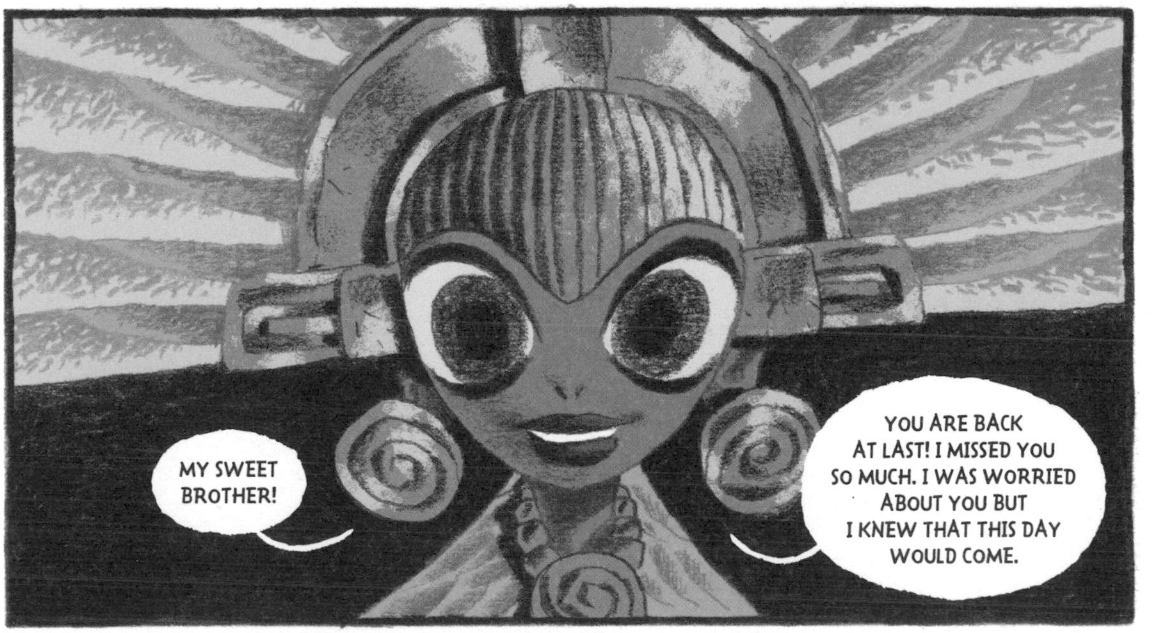
MY SWEET BROTHER!
YOU ARE BACK AT LAST! I MISSED YOU SO MUCH. I WAS WORRIED ABOUT YOU BUT I KNEW THAT THIS DAY WOULD COME.

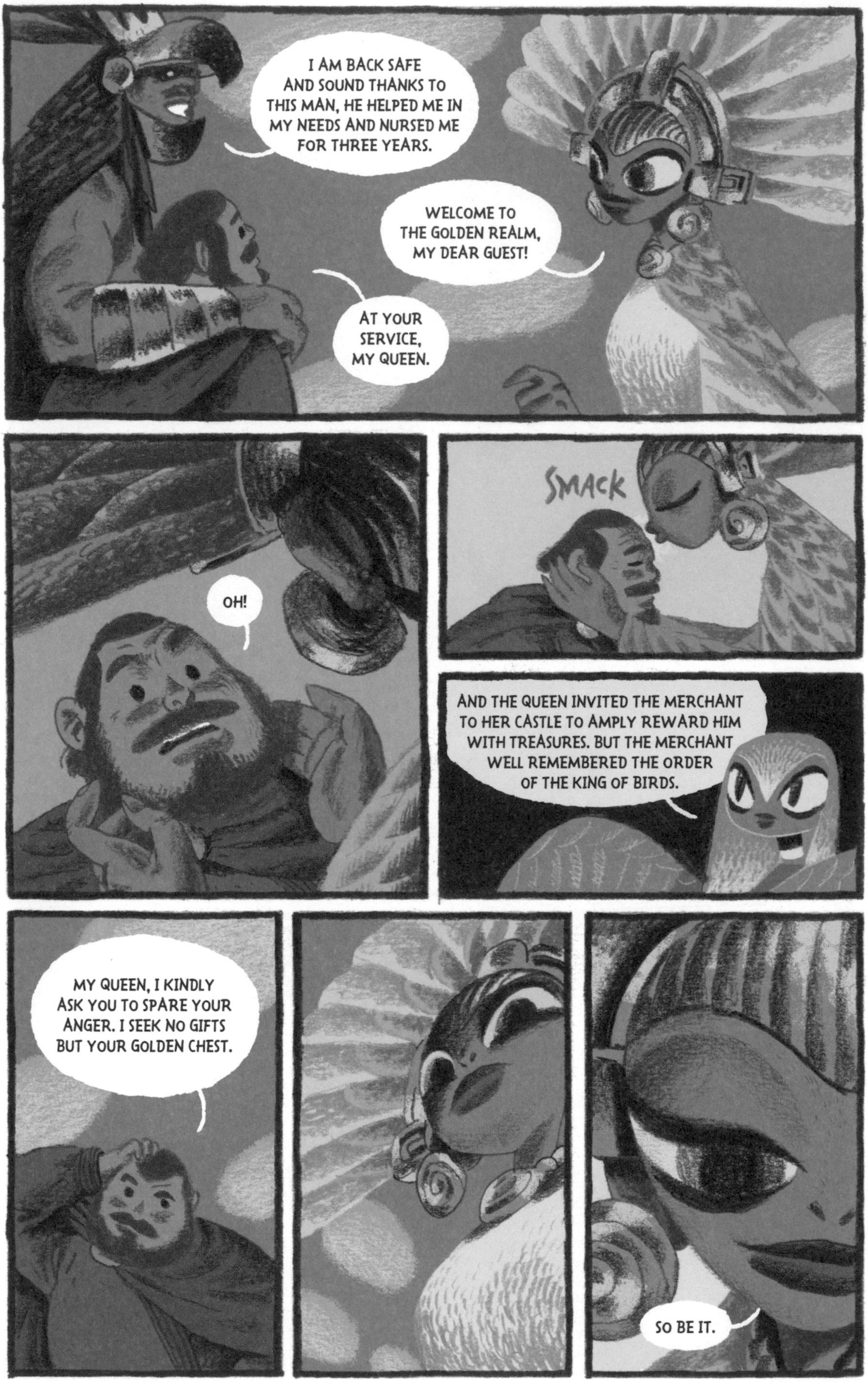
I AM BACK SAFE AND SOUND THANKS TO THIS MAN, HE HELPED ME IN MY NEEDS AND NURSED ME FOR THREE YEARS.
WELCOME TO THE GOLDEN REALM, MY DEAR GUEST!
AT YOUR SERVICE, MY QUEEN.
OH!
SMACK
AND THE QUEEN INVITED THE MERCHANT TO HER CASTLE TO AMPLY REWARD HIM WITH TREASURES. BUT THE MERCHANT WELL REMEMBERED THE ORDER OF THE KING OF BIRDS.
MY QUEEN, I KINDLY ASK YOU TO SPARE YOUR ANGER. I SEEK NO GIFTS BUT YOUR GOLDEN CHEST.
SO BE IT.

I WOULD GIVE ANYTHING FOR MY BROTHER'S SAKE!

HERE IS THE CHEST.

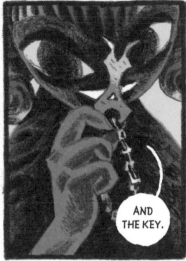

AND THE KEY.

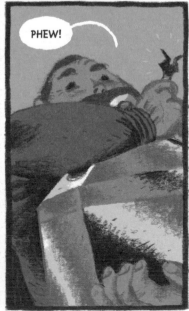

PHEW!

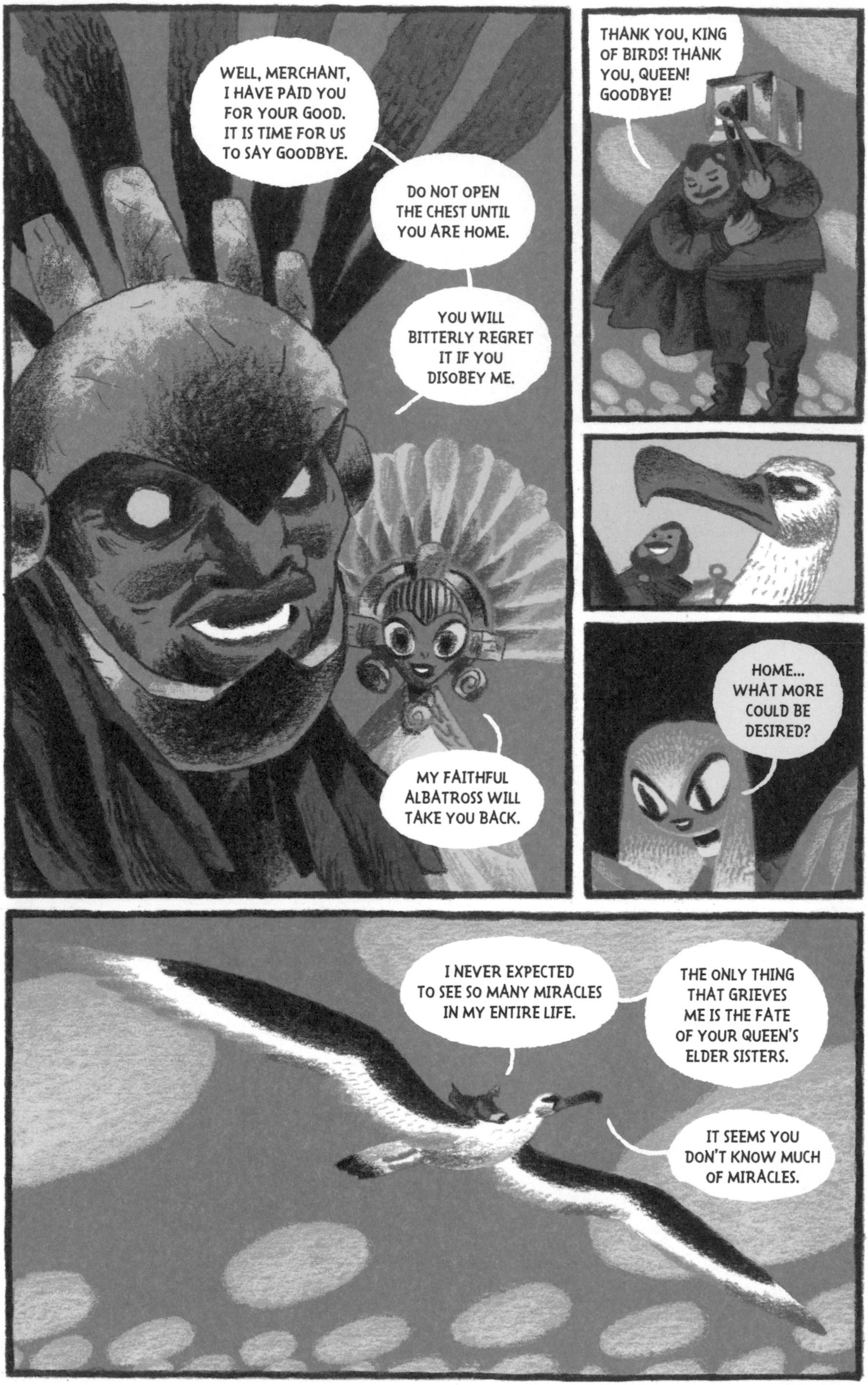
WELL, MERCHANT, I HAVE PAID YOU FOR YOUR GOOD. IT IS TIME FOR US TO SAY GOODBYE.
DO NOT OPEN THE CHEST UNTIL YOU ARE HOME.
YOU WILL BITTERLY REGRET IT IF YOU DISOBEY ME.
MY FAITHFUL ALBATROSS WILL TAKE YOU BACK.
THANK YOU, KING OF BIRDS! THANK YOU, QUEEN! GOODBYE!
HOME... WHAT MORE COULD BE DESIRED?
I NEVER EXPECTED TO SEE SO MANY MIRACLES IN MY ENTIRE LIFE.
THE ONLY THING THAT GRIEVES ME IS THE FATE OF YOUR QUEEN'S ELDER SISTERS.
IT SEEMS YOU DON'T KNOW MUCH OF MIRACLES.

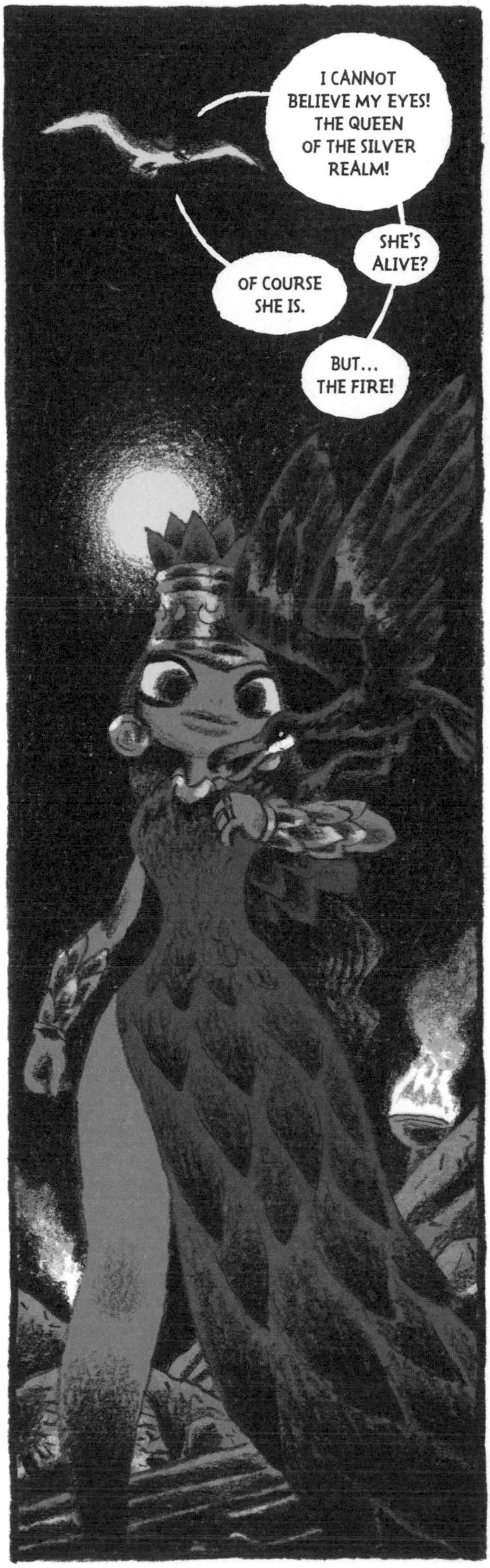
I CANNOT BELIEVE MY EYES! THE QUEEN OF THE SILVER REALM!
SHE'S ALIVE?
OF COURSE SHE IS.
BUT... THE FIRE!
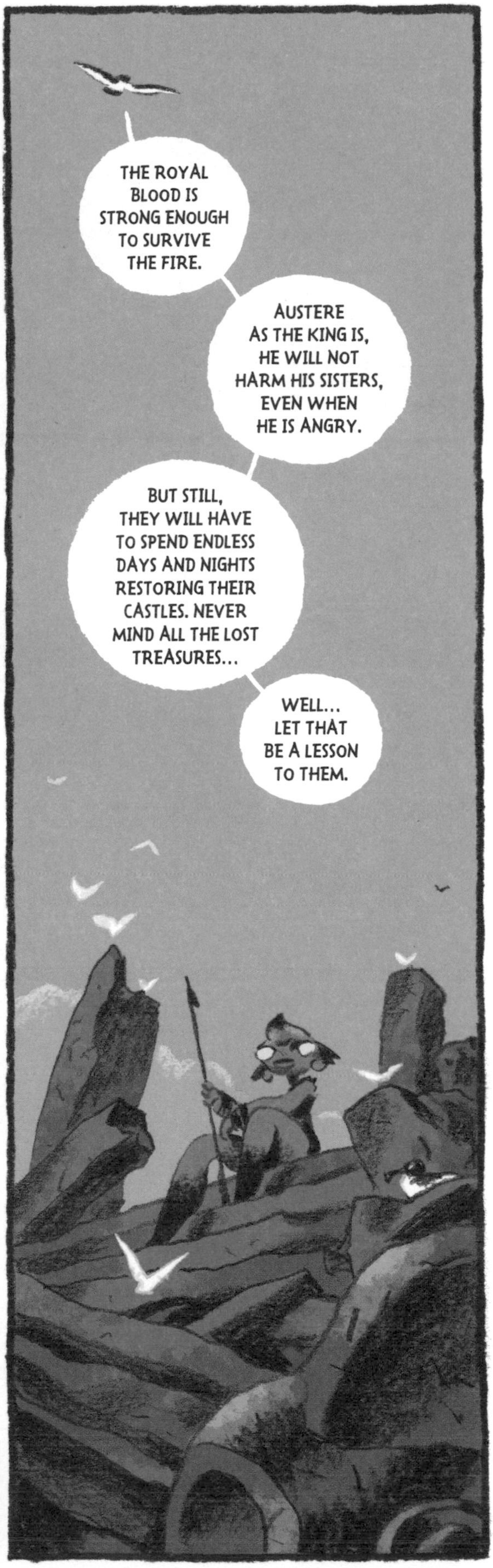
THE ROYAL BLOOD IS STRONG ENOUGH TO SURVIVE THE FIRE.
AUSTERE AS THE KING IS, HE WILL NOT HARM HIS SISTERS, EVEN WHEN HE IS ANGRY.
BUT STILL, THEY WILL HAVE TO SPEND ENDLESS DAYS AND NIGHTS RESTORING THEIR CASTLES. NEVER MIND ALL THE LOST TREASURES...
WELL... LET THAT BE A LESSON TO THEM.

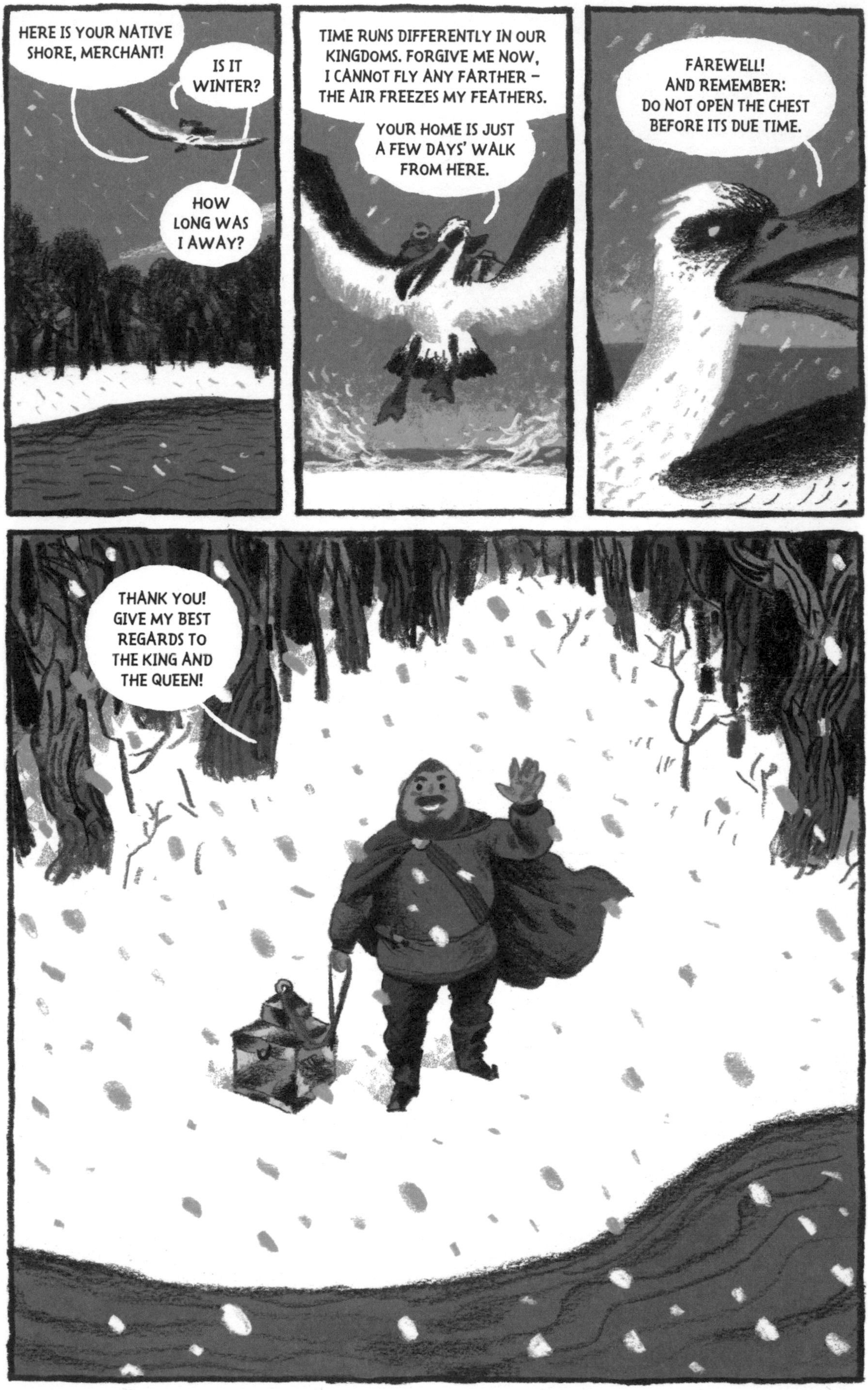
HERE IS YOUR NATIVE SHORE, MERCHANT!
IS IT WINTER?
HOW LONG WAS I AWAY?
TIME RUNS DIFFERENTLY IN OUR KINGDOMS. FORGIVE ME NOW, I CANNOT FLY ANY FARTHER – THE AIR FREEZES MY FEATHERS.
YOUR HOME IS JUST A FEW DAYS' WALK FROM HERE.
FAREWELL! AND REMEMBER: DO NOT OPEN THE CHEST BEFORE ITS DUE TIME.
THANK YOU! GIVE MY BEST REGARDS TO THE KING AND THE QUEEN!

IT IS NOT THE END

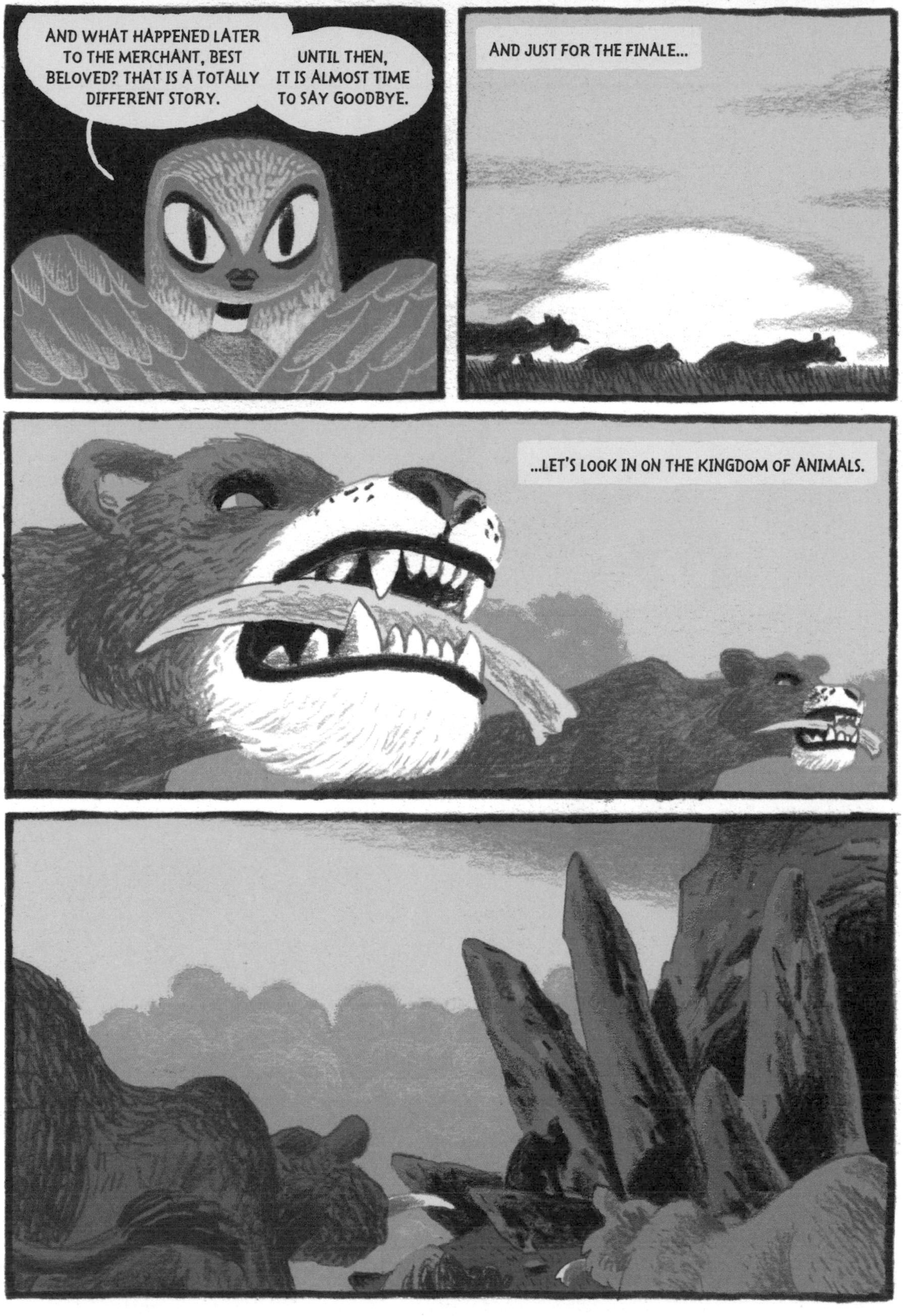
AND WHAT HAPPENED LATER TO THE MERCHANT, BEST BELOVED? THAT IS A TOTALLY DIFFERENT STORY.
UNTIL THEN, IT IS ALMOST TIME TO SAY GOODBYE.
AND JUST FOR THE FINALE...
...LET'S LOOK IN ON THE KINGDOM OF ANIMALS.

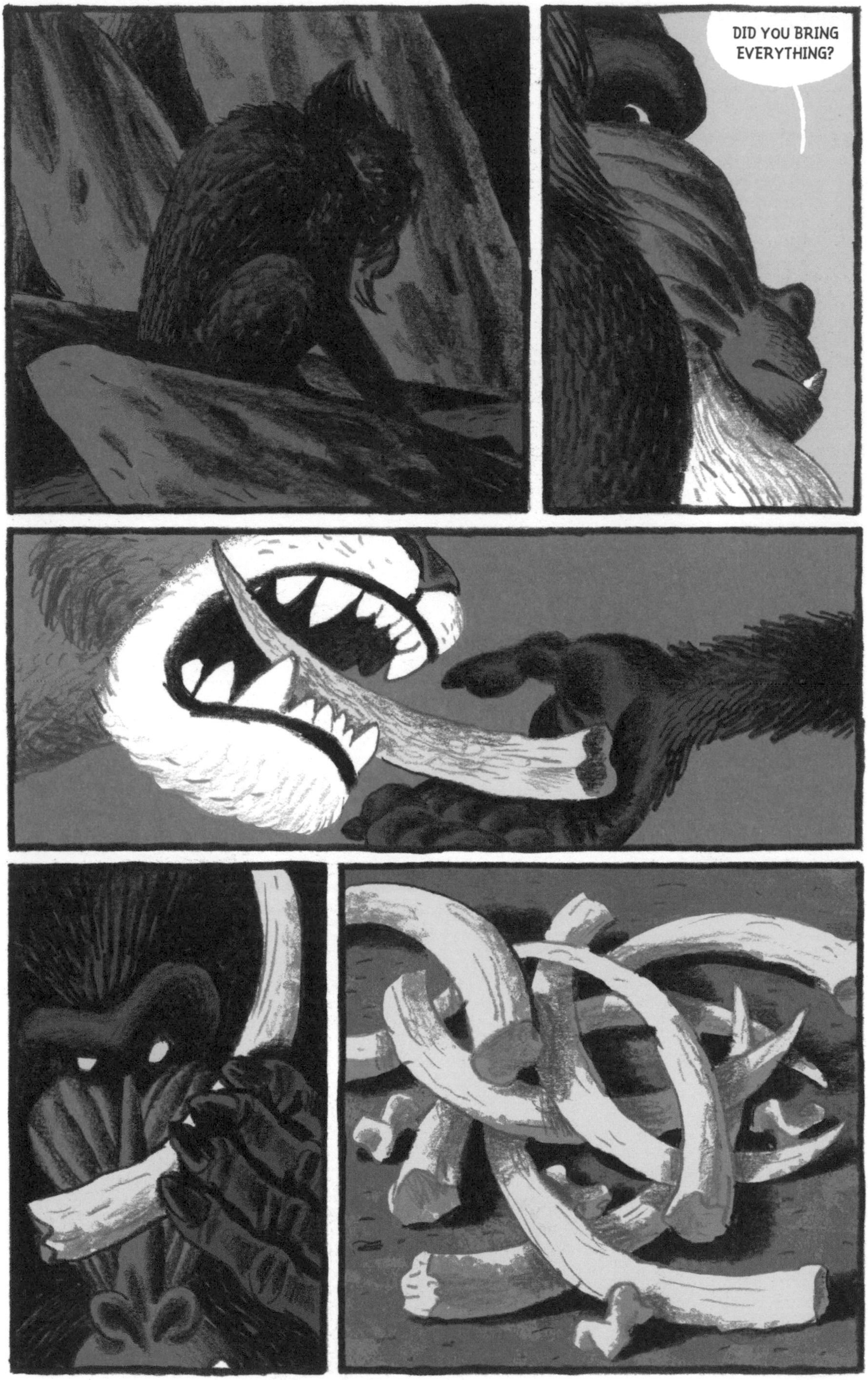
DID YOU BRING
EVERYTHING?

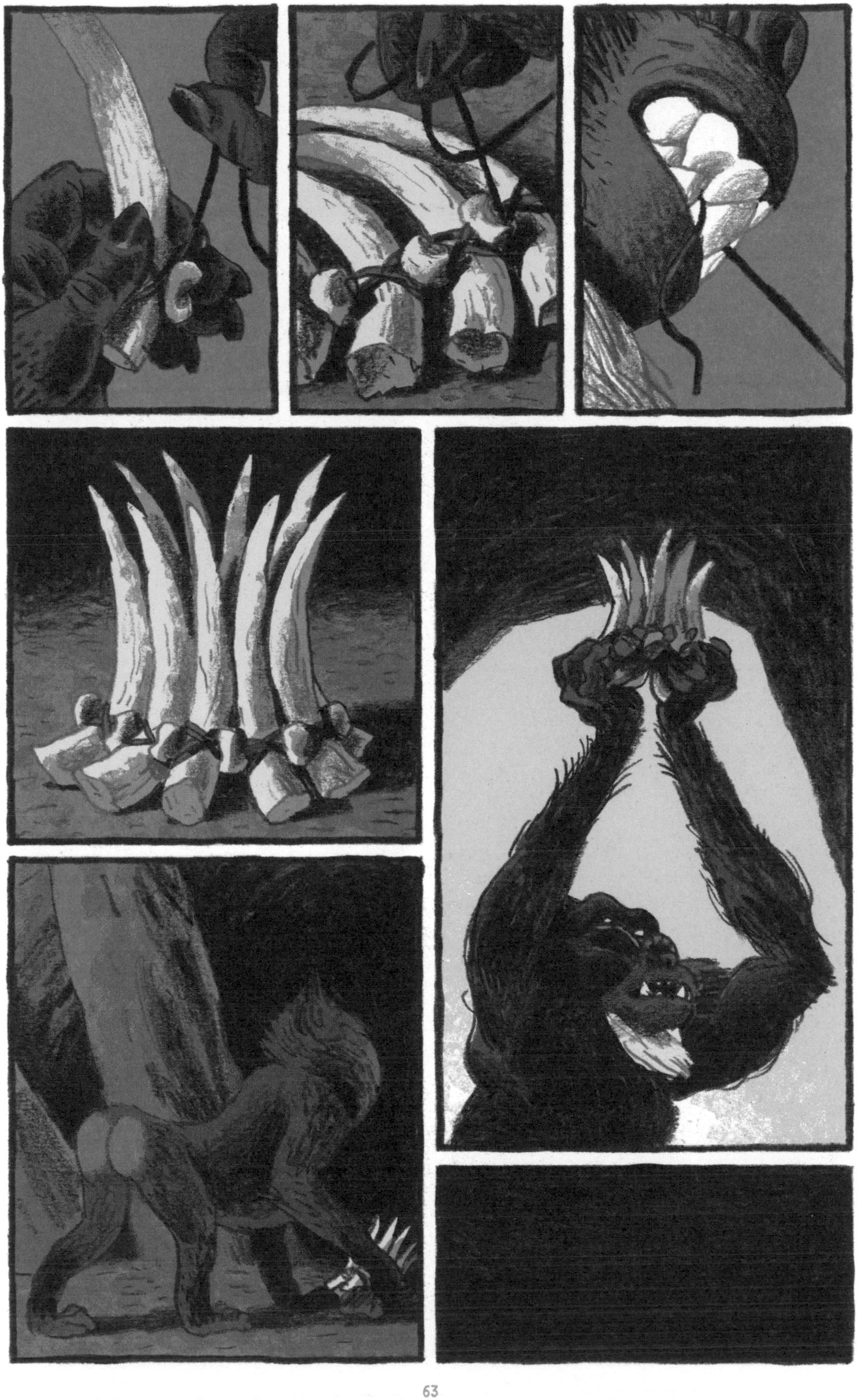

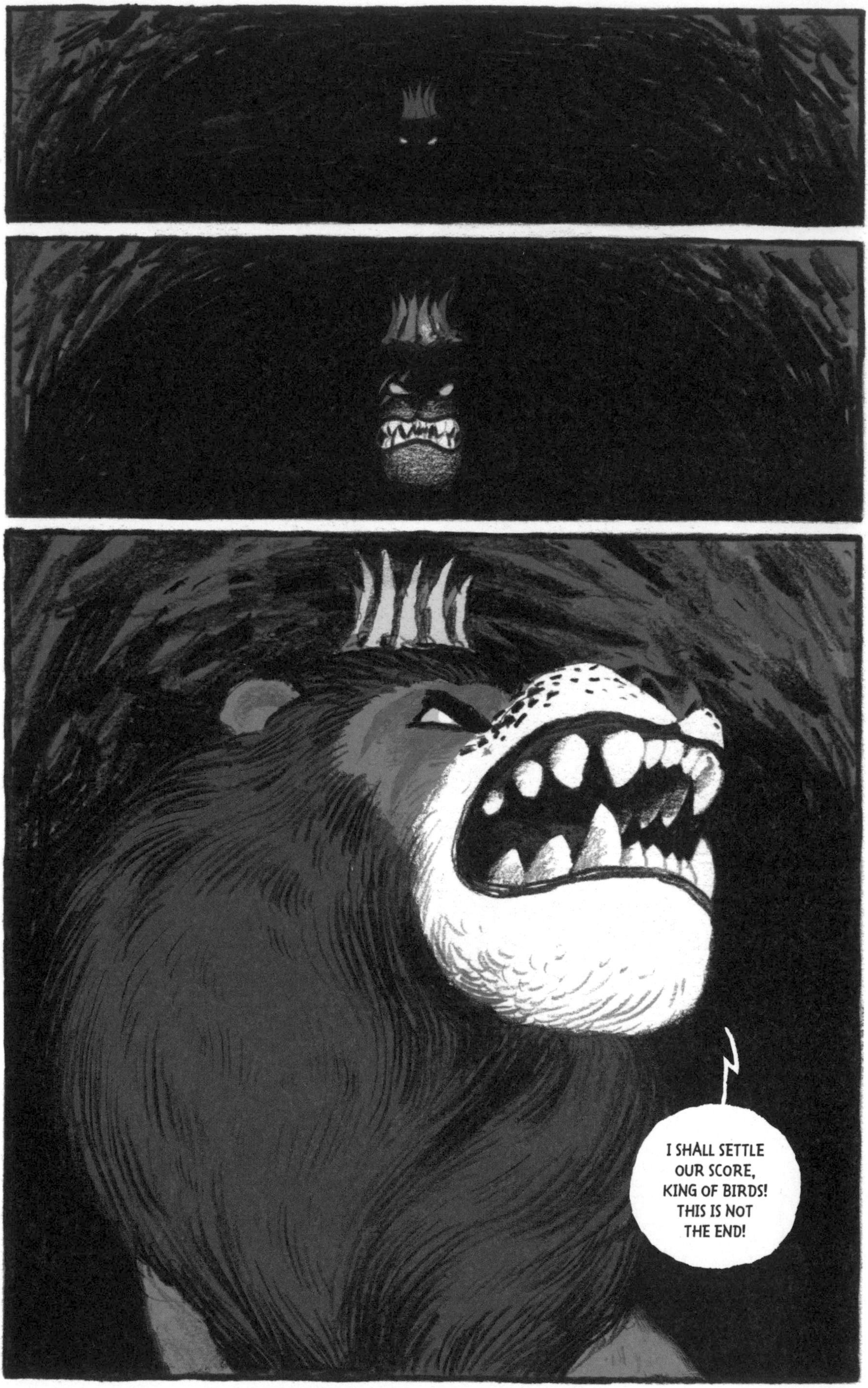
I SHALL SETTLE OUR SCORE, KING OF BIRDS! THIS IS NOT THE END!

NEXT GAMAYUN TALE:

THE WATER SPIRIT

THE MYSTERY OF THE GOLDEN CHEST IS REVEALED AND
WE MEET THE MIGHTY WATER SPIRIT, VODYANOY.
HE PLAYS HIS TRICKS WITH THE MERCHANT, WHO MUST
FACE HIS FATE WITH UNEXPECTED CONSEQUENCES...

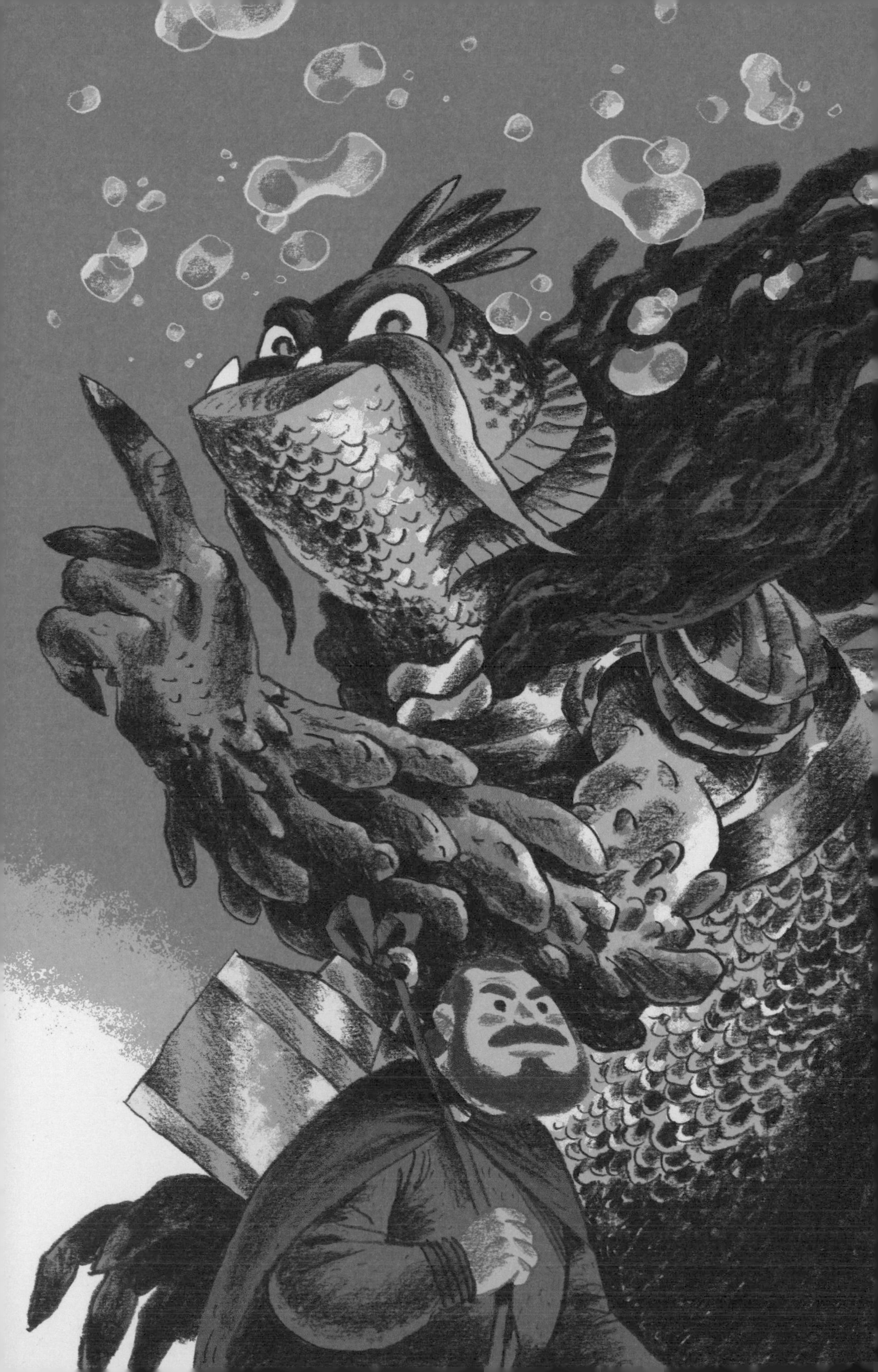

**GAMAYUN
TALES**

THE KING OF BIRDS © NOBROW 2018.

THIS IS A FIRST EDITION PUBLISHED IN 2018 BY
NOBROW LTD. 27 WESTGATE STREET, LONDON E8 3RL.

TEXT AND ILLUSTRATIONS © ALEXANDER UTKIN 2018.

TRANSLATION BY LADA MOROZOVA.

ALEXANDER UTKIN HAS ASSERTED HIS RIGHT UNDER
THE COPYRIGHT, DESIGNS AND PATENTS ACT, 1988, TO BE IDENTIFIED
AS THE AUTHOR AND ILLUSTRATOR OF THIS WORK.

PUBLISHED IN THE US BY NOBROW (US) INC.

PRINTED IN LITHUANIA ON FSC® CERTIFIED PAPER.

ISBN: 978-1-910620-38-0

ORDER FROM WWW.NOBROW.NET

'UTKIN IS A MASTER OF SHAPE AND COLOUR'

— *ANDREW MACLEAN (HEAD LOPPER, APOCALYPTIGIRL)*

'A STORY FULL OF MYSTERY, TALKING ANIMALS AND SUMPTUOUS ART THAT RIVALS AESOP'S TIMELESS TALES'

— *TROY NIXEY (JENNY FINN, THE BLACK SINISTER)*

'STYLISH AND INVENTIVE'

— *ANNA CATTISH (CHARACTER DESIGNER FOR DISNEY PUBLISHING, DREAMWORKS TV)*

'UTKIN'S FIRST BOOK IS PURE MAGIC. IT'S AS FUN, UNPREDICTABLE AND RICH AS THE RUSSIAN FOLK TALE ITSELF'

— *VICTOR MELAMED (ILLUSTRATION TEACHER, ILLUSTRATOR FOR THE NEW YORKER, ROLLING STONE AND OTHERS)*

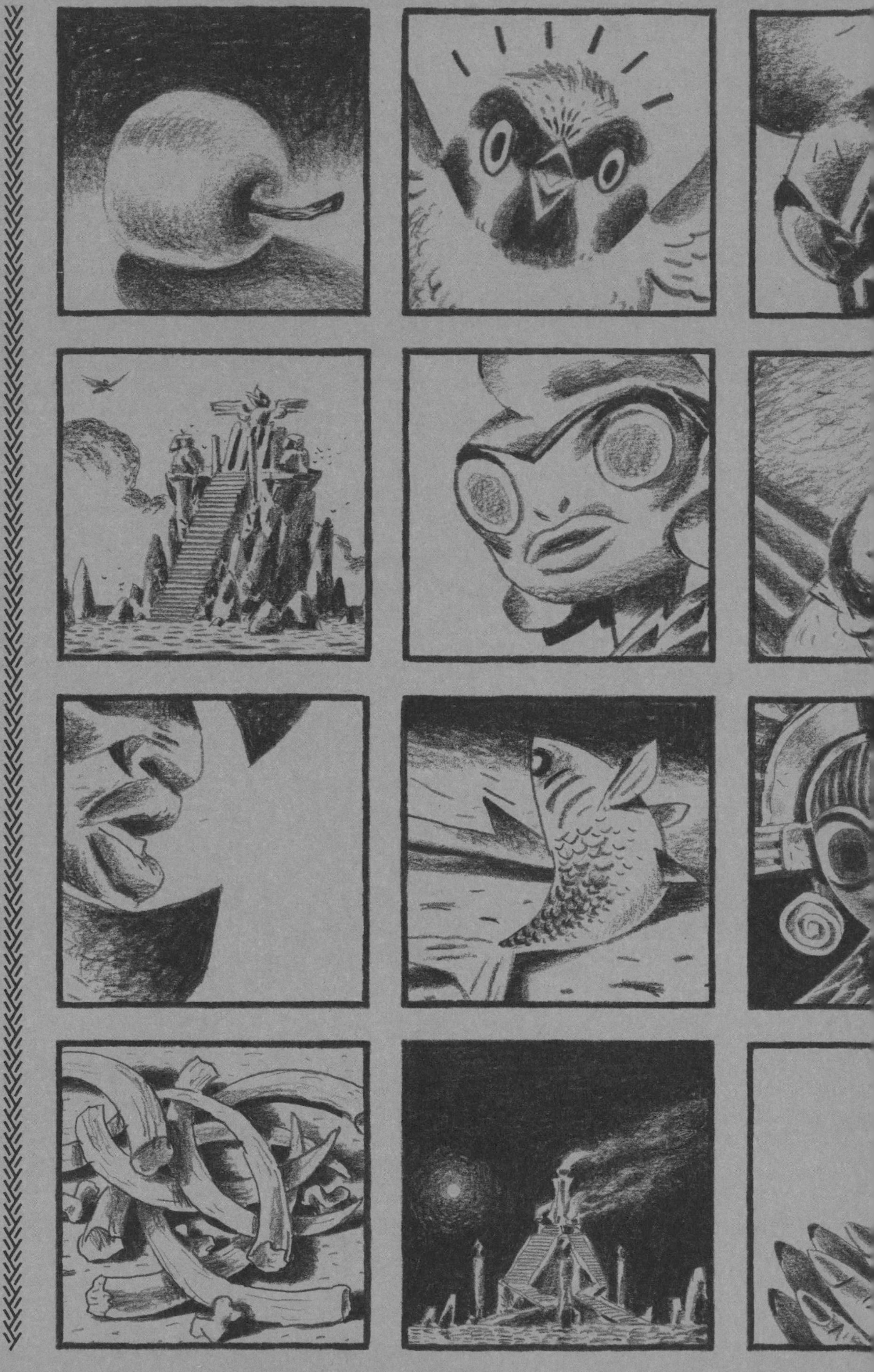